RAPUNZEL UNVEILED

USA TODAY BESTSELLING AUTHOR

ERIN BEDFORD

Also by Erin Bedford

The Underground Series
Chasing Rabbits
Chasing Cats
Chasing Princes
Chasing Shadows
Chasing Hearts
The Crimes of Alice
Hatter's Heart

The Mary Wiles Chronicles
Marked by Hell
Bound by Hell
Deceived by Hell
Tempted by Hell

Starcrossed Dragons
Riding Lightning
Grinding Frost
Swallowing Fire
Pounding Earth

The Crimson Fold
Until Midnight
Until Dawn
Until Sunset

Curse of the Fairy Tales
Rapunzel Untamed
Rapunzel Unveiled

Rapunzel Unchained

Her Angels
Heaven's Embrace
Heaven's A Beach
Heaven's Most Wanted

House of Durand
Indebted to the Vampires
Wanted by the Vampires
Protected by the Vampires
Embrace of the Vampires
Tempted by the Butler
Loved by the Vampires
Huntress of the Vampires

Academy of Witches
Witching On A Star
As You Witch
Witch You Were Here
Just Witch It
Summer Witchin'

Children of the Fallen
Death In Her Eyes
Fire In Her Blood

The Beast of the Fae Court
Granting Her Wish
Vampire CEO

RAPUNZEL UNVEILED

USA TODAY BESTSELLING AUTHOR

ERIN BEDFORD

Chapter 1

AN EIGHT-YEAR-OLD version of me looked up to the beautiful woman above me. She had the same blonde hair as me that she kept long and braided over one shoulder. Her eyes were endless pools of blue that sparkled when she smiled.

"Mommy."

"Yes, my dear Eva." Her voice was as soft as dove feathers and as light as the morning dawn. I could listen to it all day long.

Shifting in my nightgown, I slipped into my bed. The sheets were rough, but they kept me warm so I couldn't complain. "Why do the mages hate us?"

The soft smile on my mother's lips dipped slightly before she forced a brighter one to her lips. "Because they're afraid."

My eight-year-old self's brows furrowed. "Afraid?"

"Yes." She nodded solemnly. "And people who are afraid do rash and hateful things."

"But why are they afraid of us?" I asked with naive wonder. "I'd never hurt them. Would you mommy?"

Shaking her head, her braid swung back and forth. "No, of course not. But they don't know that. They don't understand us. We aren't like them."

"Because grandpa was a mage, and grandmama was human?"

She sighed. "Yes, and sadly they believe that the risk of seeing if we are good does not outweigh the need for them to feel safe."

My mouth pinched together in a pout. "That doesn't make any sense. How can we prove we aren't going to hurt them if they don't give us a chance?"

My mother laughed. The sound of it like tiny bells ringing. "That is the age-old question every king would like answered." She patted me on the head and folded me into my blankets.

Safe and warm tucked into my bed, my mother brushed my hair away from my face before pressing her lips to my forehead. "Good night, my sweet. And dream only pleasant things."

Closing my eyes, a little yawn falling from my mouth, I murmured, "Good night, Mommy."

The edges of my dream closed in around the scene, and familiar voices, ones that I had come to know, filled my head.

"We can't just leave her locked up," Luke shouted, slapping his hands on the top of Adam's desk, his white hair falling into his face. "It's not right. She hasn't done anything wrong."

Am I still dreaming?

"The council's decision is final," Gage growled through the mask covering the lower half of his face. His massive muscles flexed as they crossed over his chest while he scowled. "We cannot go against their wishes."

"You say that because you don't care about anyone outside of this family." Luke snapped, turning his angry gaze onto the stoic man.

Even if I was dreaming, it still felt good to know at least one of them was on my side.

Blake stepped up to his brother, placing his hand on his shoulder, his one good golden eye narrowing through his white and black hair. "Luke don't. She's not worth it."

Luke jerked away from Blake. "You can't mean that."

"Please," Zane interrupted, his voice calm and level as he leaned against the bookshelves. His long blood-red hair braided and hanging down the black shirt covering his chest. He pushed his glasses up his nose as he spoke. "Let us not fight among ourselves. Don't you think that is exactly what Master Tuck is trying to do?"

It was clear all of them were distressed by what happened. Well...almost all of them. If it were a dream, wouldn't I have made them all dying to let me out? To let things go back to the way they were?

"Zane is right." Adam blew out a hard breath and rubbed his forehead. "This has Master Tuck written all over it. He is dying for something to prove I'm not grand council material. We can't give him any reason to-" Adam's head jerked up, his eyes squinting at the edges. "Do you feel that?"

The others quieted and turned slightly. A tingly in the back of my mind told me they were doing something. I felt my body trying to wake and fought against it.

"Go check on, Eva," Adam ordered to no one in particular.

Luke, not surprisingly, was the one to move toward the door.

I tried to watch the others longer, but the pull to wake up was stronger now. I fought against it wanting to see something besides the four grey walls I'd stared at for the last twenty-four hours. A pounding near me was what finally did me in, jerking me awake.

My eyes flipped open, but I didn't sit up. The latch of the door clicked, and footsteps closed in behind me. The thin mattress I lay on dipped near my feet.

"Eva," Luke murmured before touching me on the shoulder. "Are you awake?"

I grunted and curled tighter into the scratchy blanket. I flashed back to the memory of my mother, and my eyes burned. I didn't remember her exactly, but the feelings seemed to have resurfaced, just like the memory.

Luke sighed heavily. "Come on, Eva. You know we didn't have a choice. If we didn't at least pretend to go along with their orders, then you'd have ended up in Master Tuck's clutches or worse." I could feel his eyes on my back, and my chest tightened with emotion. "You don't want to know what some mages do to their human servants. While there are laws against it..." he trailed off and shifted on the bed. The hand on my shoulder squeezed tight before releasing me. "I just want you to know that we didn't turn completely against you. You'll always have a place here with us."

Pain flared in my chest, and for a moment, I felt as if I were boiling alive. Rage. So much rage.

Without warning, I threw myself out of bed, throwing Luke with me. Climbing to my feet, my eyes narrowed on the man before me. In the back of my mind, I noticed the haggardness of his appearance, the stubble he hadn't shaved, the bags under his eyes, and the way his white hair was in desperate need of brushing. The rage only saw the expansiveness of his suit and robes. The clean lines and perfectly sewn golden edges. The gemstones in his medallion and ring that glinted with the light. He reeked of magic and prestige. Everything I hated. Everything I sought to destroy. Everything my mother-

"Eva," Luke reached a hand out toward me. "Are you alright? Your eyes...they're," he seemed to struggle for a word to describe them, and the one he settled on only fortified the flame. "Different."

My fingers curled into fists as I cooed, "Different? Different how? Not like you?" My feet moved to one side as I circled him. Luke twisted so he could keep track of me.

Untrusting. So afraid of what's...different.

"No, that's not what I mean at all. Eva, I -" Luke grabbed my arm, but I wrenched it back. His worried expression furrowed. "What's wrong with you?"

My head fell back, and an unfamiliar cackle forced its way out of my throat. "What's wrong with me? Why, nothing. Except for this... place." I glanced around the tiny room with distaste. My body shifted suddenly from disgust to intrigued. "Have you come to free me?" A small smile tugged on the edge of my lips, and I knew it was not a pleasant one.

Luke stared at me for a long moment as my mind struggled to take back some semblance of control.

I found my fingers walking a path along his shoulders and then grasping his already wrinkled lapels in my hands, pressing my body against his front. "Come now, I could make it worth your while."

Whatever it was that the person controlling my body expected to get from Luke did not happen and she was sorely disappointed when he pulled away from her. "I'm sorry. That's not my decision to make."

Anger flared up inside me once more, and I felt the magic billowing up before my lips formed the words. I was going to hurt Luke!

I fought harder against her control, pushing her arm down while she tried to raise it up. The words got lodged in my throat, and I must have looked a sight because Luke's expression turned to worry.

Finally, able to push my way to the surface, I cried out, "Luke! Run," before I collapsed in a heap on the floor.

Luke's arms surrounded me, keeping my head from banging on the hard floors. The scent of his musty clothes not covering his natural scent filled my nose. If I'd been able to move at all, I'd have buried my nose in the smell. Drag it into me to keep.

"Are you alright?" Luke asked after a moment of just holding me.

I huffed a breath, and my eyes fluttered open. Was I alright? I assessed my body. Nothing felt broken. Or even different. The rage inside had disappeared as did the need to hurt Luke. The only feeling left behind was sheer exhaustion.

"I think so," I licked my lips and tilted my head back to look at him. "I'm sorry. I...I don't know what came over me."

Luke brushed my hair away from my face, and after a second's hesitation, kissed my forehead. "Don't worry about it. We'll figure it out. Why don't you just rest?" Without asking if I could get up on my own, he lifted me up into his arms and laid me back onto the bed. He tucked the covers around me.

Briefly, my mind wandered back to my mother.

"Are you hungry?" Luke asked, stepping away from the bed. "I'll go get you something to eat."

I was hungry, but I couldn't help the sarcasm that came from my mouth. "Isn't that my job?"

Luke frowned. "We can talk about that later. When you're more up to it. Just rest for now."

I pulled my legs to my chest and placed my chin on my knees. "Not like I have much of a choice."

Luke paused at the doorway. "There's always a choice." And with that, he left, leaving the door wide open behind him.

I waited for about ten minutes. I held my breath for what felt like forever before I finally let my legs slip out of bed and crept toward the doorway.

When no one came rushing back shouting, "Ah-ha!" I peeked my head out of the door. A long dreary grey hallway greeted me.

Gage had dragged me down here what felt like at least a year ago, but that might be my head still not quite unfuzzy from the time in my tower. When he brought me down, I'd been too focused on not getting locked away again and did not pay much attention to my surroundings. What had felt like a shrinking room around me was an extensive tunnel system underneath the whole building.

My foot took a cautious step forward and then another. Letting my fingers trail along the wall, I followed the path to the left, figuring that was the way Luke had turned.

The lighting in the hallway wasn't like above, where massive windows were giving the place a natural look. Harsh lights that made my eyes ache burned brightly overhead. I kept my eyes down and to the side, hoping to avoid permanent damage to my eyes.

After what felt like an hour, the hallway turned. Here there were several morc doors quite like the one in my new prison. No sound came from them, but I was drawn to them, nonetheless.

Stopping at the first door, I leaned my cheek against the cold surface of it, listening to what might be inside. When nothing moved, I walked onto the next one. That one proved to be just as empty. Giving up completely, I followed the hallway until I ran into a staircase.

With my hand on the railing, I peered up the brightly lit stairway. What would be waiting for me up there? Was this a trick? Would Gage be waiting there to throw me back down and this time for good?

My heart pounded in my chest until it hurt, my hands shaking with fear.

Swallowing thickly, I pushed back my fear and made myself take that first step up and onward.

Fear made people irrational. My mother's words rang in my head. I couldn't let my fear control me.

Each step brought me closer and closer to the door at the top of the stairs. My feet were silent on the stairs, the shoes I wore proving to be worth the strange material they were made from.

When I reached the top of the stairs, I paused. My hand shook as it reached for the door handle. I clapped my other hand around my wrist, demanding it to stop it. Taking a deep breath, I wrapped my hand around the door handle and turned.

Jerking the door open, I gasped and almost fell back down the stairs. A hand rushed out and caught me about the waist, pulling me back to safety.

If my heart had been pounding before, it was about to jump out of my chest now as my eyes locked onto the tense expression of Blake, Luke's twin brother.

His single gold eye dipped over my form, surveying me for something before he scowled and released me. "Well, are you coming or not?"

He didn't wait for me to respond, turning on his heel to stalk down the hallway.

I stared after him until a yip and a wet muscle flicked at my calves.

"Izzy," I giggled and bent to pet the beast. She licked my hands and palms before rubbing herself against my lap. I scratched behind her ears and sighed. "At least someone still likes me."

With another long sigh, I stood and wandered the way Blake had gone. I suppose I should have tried to get to the front door, but the problem with that was, I didn't know how to get anywhere in Neo New York. I'd only been to a few places. The hairstylist who cut my hair. The shop where the owner had yelled at me. And the Grand Council where...I shuddered and tried to push those thoughts away. I couldn't afford to get angry right now and have another episode.

I wasn't sure what exactly had happened with Luke. It was me, but it wasn't. I knew everything I was saying and doing, but it was almost like one of my dreams. It wasn't me doing it.

It was her.

The other Eva. The one who was full of such hate and need for revenge. Just having her controlling me for that long made me need a shower. One that cleaned the inside.

Wrapping one arm around my waist, I let the other hand down where Izzy happily walked beside me. She seemed to think she was leading me, which I was perfectly fine with. The thought of having one of the others as my escort didn't appear safe right now.

Izzy led me until we stopped in front of a familiar office door.

My lips twisted to one side, and I halfheartedly glowered at the beast at my feet. "Traitor."

She yipped and scratched at the door.

Adam's voice from inside called out, "Please, come in, Eva."

Chapter 2

STEPPING INTO ADAM'S OFFICE felt about as good as getting my fingernails pulled from their roots. Not that I remembered ever having it done, but it seemed like something painful, and each step into Adam's office was just that.

The others had gone. Only Blake, Zane, and Adam remained in the room. It didn't make me feel any better.

However, Blake didn't even look away from the window when I walked in. He only moved to reach down and pet Izzy when she jumped on his crossed legs. Zane stood near the bookshelves no longer leaning but moving his finger across one of those tablet devices.

"I don't think the wards have been tampered with," Zane told Adam, the cleric's head coming up briefly to acknowledge me with an apologetic smile.

Not sure how to respond, I didn't do anything. I just stood by the door, waiting.

"Still," Adam sighed and dragged a hand through his silvery hair. "I'd feel a lot better if I knew for sure. Someone has to be watching in on us even if by non-magical means."

Zane nodded his agreement. "Of course. I will run a full diagnostic and have the house swept for bugs. If there's something here, we'll find it."

"Good." Adam stood from his desk chair and rounded the table. "Let me know either way."

Giving me one last look, Zane walked from the room, his head down engrossed with his work.

With only Blake and I left, Adam shifted his attention to me. It was a curious choice to be sure. I wished it'd been the other twin. The one who actually was on my side.

Or was he? That nagging voice in the back of my head jeered. He let the others lock you up. Why should he be any different than the rest?

"Please, have a seat." Adam gestured to the chair across from his desk and held a book in his hand. Surprisingly, it wasn't the red paperback he always seemed to be reading.

Lifting my chin in a spout of defiance, I pushed my shoulder blades back. "I'd rather stand."

Adam's expression narrowed, and I thought he might insist, but then just as quickly, he dropped it. Those brown eyes, the first pair of eyes I'd seen in over a thousand years, locked onto mine, and held it with an intensity that made me want to squirm in place.

Now I knew why Adam was the leader. He might hide behind sweetness and a polite smile, but that was how he got you in the next instance. I'd seen it in action, and yet I'd still been fooled. I wouldn't be fooled again.

Breaking the stare first, Adam glanced at the book in his hands. "It has come to my attention that we haven't been preparing you for the world outside your tower. That was my mistake." He flipped a page. "I treated you as if you knew you were one of us, but the truth is, you're not." Another page flipped.

My fingers curled into fists, and my jaw clenched. "What gave you that idea?"

Adam paused in his flipping, his head abruptly jerking up. "Not that I do not enjoy that pert mouth of yours, but comments like that will have to stop. At least, until we know the threat is gone." He paused and went back to flipping the pages. I didn't think he was even reading the damnable book.

I snorted.

Clipping the book shut, Adam leaned back against his desk, the book sitting in front of his lap. "Do you think this makes me happy?" He tilted his head to one side, watching me with a pained expression. "Do you think I want to be this guy? We don't have humans here in our house for a reason."

"No one would put up with us," Blake grumbled from the window, his fingers scratching at Izzy's chin.

Adam shot Blake a glare before turning back to me. "As Blake not so eloquently stated, not many humans want to work for five mages, let alone male ones."

"I didn't realize they had a choice in the matter." I crossed my arms and cocked my hip, unable to keep the attitude out of my voice. "I thought they're born and thrown to whatever mage family needs or wants someone." As if humans were just animals to pass around as they liked.

Scoffing, Adam pushed off the desk and approached me. "We are not so barbaric as all that. It's not like we have a human trading market or something. We certainly don't just give humans to mages. Humans are employed by the families they work for. They are given wages as well as a home and protection."

He paused when he was but a foot before me. Those brown eyes hardened as he frowned down at me.

"There are strict rules and regulations that must be followed when caring for a human. Those who break those rules are just as harshly punished as humans who step out of line."

To my surprise, he reached a hand toward me and slid his fingers through the lengths of my hair, his eyes softening. "The majority of us are not the sadistic creatures you must have conjured up in your room last night."

I stepped away from him, making his hand drop. "My jail cell, you mean."

Adam lifted his eyes to the ceiling, muttering something under his breath before turning back to his desk. "That room was one in the servants' corridors. Since we obviously never intended to employ a human, we didn't bother with furnishings or making it...comfortable." He rounded his desk and plopped down in his chair, and Adam threw his booted feet up on the edge of it. "We'll get you some proper furnishings, and you won't even know the difference between it and your room before."

I couldn't help it. Adam seemed so sure of himself. So confident that he was doing me a favor. I laughed.

After a few moments, my laugh turned to hysteria, causing both Blake and Adam to stare at me. Izzy yipped and bounded over to my side, peering up at me curiously as her tail beat against the floor.

"Is this part of her being crazy or..." Blake asked Adam shifting off the windowsill and approached us slowly, his one gold eye watching me.

"I'm not quite sure. Eva?"

I waved their concern off, my laughter cutting off at once. "I'm quite sane. For the moment. But if you," I pointed my finger at Adam, "think you are doing any human a favor by putting them in the basement where there are no windows, no way to the outdoors, then you are kidding yourself." I shook my head, and I felt the hysteria building again. "I might have been out of my mind and locked in a tower for hundreds of years, but even I had a window. Even if I couldn't see out of it."

Adam visibly relaxed. "Oh. Is that all it is? We can easily have a window put in."

I frowned my brows drawing together at his flippant response. "Have a window put in...in the basement?"

Ignoring my question, Adam turned Blake. "Can you have your brother help you with the specifics? I've never added a window to an underground room. Still, it can't be too much more complicated than altering the basic composition of the house."

Blake nodded. "It'll have to be a mirrored window. Since there wouldn't be anywhere for the window to actually look out to.

Perhaps one from the second floor?" His gaze shifted to me. One of his brows arched.

If he expected me to answer him, he would be sorely disappointed. I had no clue what they were talking about, let alone have an opinion.

"That should be fine," Adam answered for me, before switching his attention back to me. "As for you, Eva. We must begin your training at once. Most humans go to a school to learn all the basic needs for serving a mage, but you'll have to settle for us." His lopsided grin was meant to be encouraging, I was sure, but it only made me want to hit him.

The whole thing was ridiculous. I didn't have time to learn to be a servant. I had to figure out who I was and why I had magic. Then I had to get as far away from the lot of them before I ended up being experimented on. An image of the mage back at the headquarters made me want to vomit. He had wanted to pick me apart and see how I worked, no matter if I died in the process, and that was just from surviving a stasis spell for so long.

"First, I think a change of clothes and a nice bath would be in order? Then maybe some breakfast?" Adam arched a brow but didn't wait for me to answer. "I'll have Luke help you-"

"No!"

Adam and Blake shot me a surprised look.

I hurried to follow it up with, "I mean, no. I don't need help getting changed and cleaned up. I still know how to do those things myself. Just tell me what you want me to wear." I didn't want to see Luke. Not after what happened a bit ago.

The other Eva seemed to come out when she felt like she'd been betrayed, and I didn't need to reflect too far to know that Luke was at the top of my list of betrayers. Even if he was a reluctant participant.

"Blake."

"Got it. I'll find her something." Blake answered Adam's unspoken request with his gaze searching my face the entire time.

"Very well."

Once Blake had left the room taking Izzy with him, Adam focused his attention on me. Well, partly. That red book of his appeared in his hand again. "Now, Eva," Adam began, his eyes lazily skimming the page as he spoke. "Since we don't know the exact extent of your abilities, I thought we might start with something easy."

"Easy?" I shifted in place, not liking the sound of that.

"You and Zane discovered you're from the middle ages, and you had to eat then, correct?"

"Yes?" I drew out curious to see where he was going with this. "I suppose I would."

"Then, it only makes sense that you would know how to cook."

Based on how lavish and poised other Eva was, I had a hard time believing she had ever peeled a potato in her life. However, I couldn't very well tell Adam that. Instead, I shrugged. "I don't know, but we can give it a try."

"Good." He bobbed his head and headed toward the door, his eyes still down in his book. "I'll meet you in the kitchen when you've changed."

Before I could answer, he was out the door.

Well. Then.

I crossed my arms over my chest and huffed for a moment. I hated this. It was apparent now that the mages weren't happy with this situation any more than I was, which did make being locked away sting a tiny bit less but only a little. However, the way they were acting toward me now, all short and to the point, hurt.

Before all this craziness with the council, they'd treated me nicer like one of them, and I had felt safe and happy for the first time in... well ever. If this was how we were going to be from now on, I didn't think I could handle it.

While I'd been alone and out of my mind in the tower, at least I wasn't in danger of getting my feelings hurt. The way each of them looked at me now made my chest sting and tighten. I wanted a family. I wanted my mother. Though I couldn't remember much of her, from what I knew, she had been wonderful.

I sucked in a sharp breath and pushed the tears back. I had to be strong. I couldn't let myself fall down that hole. I had a hard enough time keeping the other Eva back before, I couldn't give her any openings.

Unfortunately, the turn of events didn't look promising. Not with the way they were treating me. One thing I knew from watching the other Eva was she did not like mages. Not one bit.

Chapter 3

I SHIFTED UNCOMFORTABLY IN my new clothes. Though, new was debatable. The ugly grey of the plain dress made it nearly impossible to tell if someone else had owned the dress before me. Its plain design and the long hem was a far cry from the lovely blue dress I'd been wearing. At least, they let me keep the shoes.

"How does it fit?" Blake quirked a brow, standing off to one side. Izzy yipped and bounced around at our feet.

I twisted one way and then the other, my face scrunching tightly. "It itches." Izzy growled as if it offended her as well.

Blake shrugged. "It's a basic uniform. All the others wear the same thing."

My brows rose. "And have you ever asked them how they felt about that?"

Blake frowned and seemed thoughtful. "I wouldn't know. I've never had a human in my house before."

This had my attention. "Never? Not even when you lived with your parents."

Blake's single golden eye grew dark. "No. My parents died when Luke and I were five."

My hand came to my mouth, and I took a step toward him. "Oh, I'm so sorry. I didn't know."

"Of course, you wouldn't." Blake snapped that wall back up in place as if he had never let me peek over it. "If you're done complaining, Adam is waiting and I'm hungry, so get going." He didn't wait for me to follow him out of the room before he stalked away.

I stared down at Izzy with a frown. "One day I'm going to get that one to like me."

Izzy thumped her long tail against the floor and yipped.

"Izzy! Come."

I shook my head with a smile. "I have a feeling I should get used to that kind of call as well." I followed the hell hound out of the room, looking to her as we walked. "Any advice?"

She stopped and scratched behind her ear.

"Should I know what that means?"

Izzy yipped again and bounded after some invisible fiend. Sighing, I trailed after her down the narrow hallway. One of these days, I might get used to the dankness of the basement, but that day wasn't today.

I wanted to be outside and feel the breeze on my face and the heat of the sun on my skin. Not stuck in the ground as if I were already dead and buried.

Pushing the morbid thoughts away, I held my itchy skirt up as I walked up the stairs. Izzy had chased after whatever it was she had seen, and Blake was nowhere to be found. I was on my own for once, and I had mixed feelings about it.

My eyes shifted toward the hallway, the one which would lead me to the kitchen, and then to the other way, where the front door stood.

For a moment, I thought about leaving.

I could just up and leave. Go back to my tower. Or...not. I'd go somewhere. Anywhere else.

Then I glanced down at my clothing. I couldn't do that dressed like a servant. They'd just send me right back here or worse...I shuddered.

Besides, even if I had new clothes, I still smelled human. The mages would be able to tell, and I'd be back at the beginning once again.

Letting out a long sigh, I pivoted down the hallway, toward the kitchen, and what may just be the rest of my life.

When I arrived in the kitchen, I was surprised to see Adam standing at the middle counter wearing a frilly white apron. He had a different book in his hand this time. This one with a large basket of fruits and vegetables on the front.

I had a thought.

"Do you even know how to cook?"

Adam lowered the book to meet my gaze over the top. "Of course, I do. I can't very well teach you if I couldn't. Now, can I?"

I shrugged, approaching the counter to lean my arms over it. "How should I know?

For all I know, you don't know the difference between a *Chykonys in Bruette* and a *Gelyne in Brothe*?"

Adam lowered the book entirely, arching a brow at me, his lovely lips curling at the edges. "How do you know the difference?"

"Of course, one is chicken in ale broth, and the other is hen..." I trailed off as Adam stared at me.

How did I know that?

"Well, that's comforting to know." Adam stepped from the counter and over to the cold box. Refrigerator that was the word they used. I needed to remember that.

"What is?"

"You obviously know something about the culinary arts, or else you wouldn't have even known what to compare." He withdrew from the...refrigerator and sat down several items on the counter.

My lips twisted to one side as I looked over the items. Milk, eggs, peppers, and cheese.

"What's wrong?"

"I'm just wondering why you even cook?"

Adam stopped what he was doing, placing the board on the counter. "What do you mean?"

"Well," I huffed, coming around the counter to where the machine that made coffee sat. "You have all these fancy devices, and you don't have a single one that cooks for you?"

Adam chuckled. "Oh. Well..." he scratched the back of his head and then walked the few feet over to the stove. He reached into a cabinet and pulled out a little clear bottle. Popping the top, he poured a handful into his hand. Small different colored balls sat in the palm of his hand.

I leaned over his hand and then reached for one of the balls.

"Go ahead," Adam urged me when I hesitated. "They're perfectly safe."

I picked up a pale blue ball and held it up to the light. I couldn't see inside it, and it wasn't heavy. "What is it?"

"Dehydrated meals." Adam held the bottle up for me to see. "Just pop one in the microwave and push the rehydrate button, and you have a full meal right there."

I pursed my lips and glowered at him. "Then why do I need to cook?"

Adam gave a nervous chuckle. "Well, you see. They're fine for when you're in a pinch, but if you eat them too regularly, they cause constipation."

My brows drew together. "Oh. But then why don't you just use magic to make your food?"

Adam took the blue ball from my fingers and popped it back into the bottle. Putting it back into the counter, he explained, "All magic has a cost. Even for food." Closing the cabinet, he turned back to me and held out a hand. A shiny red apple appeared in it. "We can't make something from nothing. It has to come from somewhere."

Before I could ask a question, a shout of anger and then feet stopping on the floor interrupted us. Gage appeared in the doorway. His eyes searched the room and then zeroed in on the apple in Adam's hand. "That's mine."

Adam gave him an apologetic smile. "Sorry, friend. I needed an example." He tossed the apple to Gage.

"Use someone else next time." Gage caught the apple in midair and stalked back out of the room.

Smiling, Adam said, "See? Can't get something for nothing."

"That doesn't mean you couldn't cook up something magically with what you have here in the kitchen," I pointed at the items on the counter.

"True." Adam inclined his head. "But most mages see that as a waste of their abilities." I snorted and rolled my eyes. Adam added on with a mischievous wink. "Magic food always ends up with a chalky aftertaste anyway."

I sighed. "Fine. What are we making?"

Adam and I approached the counter, and he held out the red and green bell peppers. "I thought we could make something easy, perhaps a quiche."

I took the peppers and stared at them. "What's a quiche?"

"Sort of like a cake or tart. You mix eggs with whatever you want to go in it. You could put vegetables or meats in it, but you have to chop them into small bits, or the quiche won't stay together right." Adam shifted from the counter to the refrigerator and then paused. "You're not allergic to anything, are you?"

"Allergic?"

He frowned and then said, "There aren't any foods that make you sick?"

"Oh!" I thought for a moment. "Not that I know of? I guess we'll find out."

Adam chuckled, "I suppose we will," as he pulled out some mushrooms from the box as well. "Just if your tongue starts to feel big and fat, let me know."

"Uh. Okay?"

We took the vegetables to the sink and rinsed them off. Adam's shoulder brushed and bumped against mine as we took turns cleaning the peppers and mushrooms. I became more and more alert to how close he was to me, and it made my heart race.

When we finished, I cleared my throat, taking a step back. "Now what?"

"Now," Adam picked up the cleaned vegetables and moved to the middle counter where he'd placed the wooden block. "We cut them." He pulled out a knife from a drawer and held it out to me. "Let's see what you've got."

I cautiously stepped up beside him, taking the knife he offered. Holding the knife gently in my hand, I stared down at the vegetables. I didn't know where to begin cutting them. Did I half them? Or were you supposed to start at the end?

"Here," Adam stepped up behind me, his arms wrapping around me. His warm hands covered mine, shifting the red pepper into place and lifting the knife.

I hardly breathed while he steered my hands to cut the pepper down the middle longways.

"You have to clean the seeds out before cutting it smaller." Adam's voice grew lower as he used two fingers to scoop the seeds off the sides. I picked up the other piccc and began mimicking his movements. Soon they were both completely clean, and Adam stepped away from me.

I took that moment to take deep breaths before he came back over with a wet cloth. I held my hand out without being asked and almost fainted as he stroked the damp cloth up and down my fingers.

"There." He smiled faintly. "We wouldn't want to accidentally touch your lovely eyes and burn them."

I stared at him and nodded humbly, swallowing a thick lump in my throat. "Yeah." I cleared my throat and turned back to the counter. "So, uh, does it matter how I cut them?"

Adam, much to my disappointment, stood beside me rather than behind me as he gestured toward the two halves. "Not really. Just make sure they're small enough to fit into a muffin pan."

When I stared blankly at him, Adam quickly moved to a cabinet and withdrew a slab of metal with small dips in them. "This is a muffin pan."

"Oh."

He placed it on the stove and then sat down on a stool across from me at the counter. A part of me was thankful for the distance, but another half wanted him close again.

Pushing the thoughts back, I focused on the task at hand. I cut the pepper into long strips and then into even smaller cubes. When that was done, I looked at Adam for approval. He nodded.

I continued to do the same thing for the other peppers, cleaning and seeding them before cutting them up. Then came the mushrooms.

While I was washing them, I had my back to Adam. He hadn't said much while I cut the rest of the vegetables, but I could feel his eyes on me the whole time. Even now, they bore into my back and made me shift in place.

It wasn't that I didn't like the attention. On the contrary, I probably liked it a bit too much. Just being close to the chipper man made my insides do a strange sort of dance. But I also couldn't forget that behind those smiles and compliments were a man who could turn on you in an instant. He'd shown me as much just less than twenty-four hours ago.

"Oh!" I cried, jumping in place as a hand slipped around my waist.

"I think they've been washed enough, don't you?" Adam's hot breath caressed the side of my neck, and I bit my lip to hold back the sounds threatening to come out.

Realizing what he'd said, I glanced down at the mushrooms and laughed nervously. "Oh, yes. I suppose they are clean." I turned the water off and spun around the bowl of mushrooms in my hands. It worked as a sad buffer between Adam and me.

Those intense brown eyes stared into mine without saying anything at first. Then, Adam's hand lifted. "Your hair."

"What about it?" I forced my head to stay still and not lean into his touch as his fingers trailed along the surface of my pale locks.

"You really should tie it back when you cook." He pushed my hair from either side of my shoulder, using one hand to hold it behind my head snuggly.

I couldn't breathe.

This was ridiculous! I'd never reacted this way before, or at least, I didn't remember doing so. The way he looked at me with such ferocity and the stronghold on my hair did something to me. It made my insides burn and my mouth dry. I had a sudden need for him to tug on my hair just a bit more.

Adam's gaze shifted from my face and down to my heaving chest. His face was hard to read, but I wanted nothing more than to know what he was thinking at that very moment. Was he as affected as I was? Did his pulse jump, and his nipples pebble from just being close?

His head dipped down, and my hand went to his chest, the bowl of mushrooms falling to the floor with a clatter. The sound broke whatever spell Adam was under.

Releasing my hair, he stepped away from me, putting several feet between us before his eyes dropped to the mushrooms on the floor.

To distract myself from what almost happened again, like the first time he almost kissed me in his office, I dropped to my knees and scrambled to pick up the mushrooms.

A sharp inhale from Adam had me looking up from my place on the ground. From this position, I could quite clearly see the bulge in the front of his pants.

So, he *was* as affected as me.

It was nice to know, but it didn't make their predicament any better. I was still a human with a secret and him the grandson of the Arch Mage, the leader of the council of mages. For us to get involved more than we already were wouldn't be good for any of us. Least of all me, when the other Eva wanted nothing more than to dig her claw into any mage she could find, ripping them from the inside out.

"What's wrong?" The concern instead of desire in Adam's voice startled me out of my thoughts.

I hurried to pick up the rest of the mushrooms and stood, making sure not to touch him as I went back to the counter. "Nothing. Just thinking."

"What about?" Adam didn't return to his seat, standing much too close to me for comfort.

I began to cut the mushrooms with quick movements, my words coming out forced and hard. "I'm trying to figure out not only who I am but where I fit into this world and you..." I paused to point the knife at him as I grunted my frustration. "You are making things confusing."

Adam frowned. "I'm sorry. I didn't mean to make things more difficult for you." I turned my attention back to the cutting, unable to bear the kindness in his gaze. "I've tried." His voice went low and soft. "I've tried to keep my eyes to myself. To keep my hands busy, though, they want nothing more than to stroke your hair and hold you close." He cursed under his breath and pounded on the table.

I startled, and a sharp pain slit through my finger. "Ah!"

"Oh, Eva!" Adam reached for the hand I'd cut, producing a cloth from thin air. "I shouldn't have. Ugh. I can't seem to think straight around you." He gave me a weak smile as he pressed the cloth against my finger to still the bleeding. "I'm to be the next

Arch Mage, and here I am acting like a lovesick fool." His eyes dropped to my hand. "You talk of complications. You don't even know the half of it. I should never have...even to think of taking a human for a lover would cause such a mar on my record I couldn't even show my face to the council again, let alone run it."

I swallowed hard and nodded. As much as I didn't like it, I understood.

Humans were seen as beneath them. I didn't know a lot about this world but that, I knew. From what I read in the books about the time I was from, it would be the equivalent of a king taking a milkmaid as his mistress. Sure, it could be overlooked if it were just one time, but to give them such a position would upset the whole hierarchy. Adam couldn't risk that with me.

"I think it has stopped bleeding." Adam wrapped the cloth around my finger tightly. "I'll finish up here. You should have Luke heal it. I think he's in the-"

"No." I shook my head. "It's fine. I don't need healing."

"But Eva," Adam began, concern crossing his features. "It could get infected. You really should have it healed."

My eyes burned as they bore into Adam's. "Not him."

Adam didn't say anything at first and then nodded solemnly. "Very well. Zane knows something about the healing arts. He's likely in the chapel."

Chapter 4

ADAM WALKED ME TO the chapel, his gaze on his red book. Not speaking, he made sure to keep his distance from me.

If he hadn't told me why he couldn't be with me, then I'd have been offended. As it was, it still stung.

"I think I'm good here."

We stopped at the door of the chapel. I wrapped my arms around my waist, my eyes dropping to the ground. I couldn't bear to see Adam's face. It would only make his rejection of me harder.

"Are you sure?" Adam reached a hand out to me, and I backed away, my back smacking the door.

"Yes. I'll be-" I lost control of my mouth as words I hadn't ever thought I'd say to Adam came pouring out. "Great as soon as I'm away from the likes of you."

"Eva?"

My eyes narrowed, and my lips twisted in disgust. "Why would I want to be kissed by a backstabbing elitist mage?"

Adam's eyes widened.

"You don't deserve the magic you have," I spat at him. My fingers curled into tight fists, not caring about the pain in my finger now. "You let the humans rot while you play at being heroes rescuing the damsel in a tower only to try and make her one of the miserable creatures you claim to have saved too. But if you go out there," I shoved a finger toward the hallway, "and ask any of them how grateful they are, I bet not even one would thank you."

The sad and shameful expression on Adam's face as he clipped his book close with a sigh snapped me out of it.

I clamped my hands over my mouth, wincing as the pain came roaring back. "Adam, I'm so sorry."

"Don't." His face drooping as he spoke. "You're right. The mages, me, act like we have made the world a better place. Saving humans from themselves. When really, we've just exchanged one hell for another."

I reached for him, taking a step forward. "Adam..."

Adam straightened and sniffed, his eyes filling with determination. "That's why I have to become Arch Mage. So I can fix what we've done." He took the last few steps, closing the distance between us. Adam gripped my shoulders and drew me close, kissing me hard on the mouth before jerking back to whisper harshly. "No one will keep me from that goal. Not even my desire for you."

Pushing away from me, Adam stalked down the hallway, not giving me a second look.

The fingers of my uninjured hand traced my lips. I was getting kissed an awful lot lately. It made me wonder if the other Eva was ever this popular. Something told me she was, but no one probably dared to kiss her unless she said so, and even then, they might be risking their life.

With a sigh, I pulled open the chapel door, wondering when my life got so complicated. Things were so much simpler back in my tower.

What makes you think you're not still there?

I frowned.

"That's an unhappy expression."

My head turned to where Zane stood by the front of the chapel near a rose bush, a watering can in his hands. My gaze slid over his form as a small smile tugged at my lips.

Zane had removed his outer jacket and had the black sleeves of his shirt rolled up to his elbows. He'd pulled his blood-red hair up on top of his head in a high ponytail, giving him a more rakish look. As he bent to water the roses, the long-chain holding the mages Crest, a red tree branch bent into a cross, hung down between the opening of the shirt. Between the edges, I could just make out the black lines of the sigil tattooed on his chest.

My hand itched.

I'd touched that sigil before. The power that had radiated out of me from a single command had scared and exhilarated me. It had kept the demon lurking inside of Zane at bay but had also shown me I was more than just an ordinary human.

"I have a lot on my mind." I offered him another weak smile as I moved along the stone path.

Zane inclined his head. "I can imagine you do. This is quite a change for you and so suddenly. It's only normal you would be discombobulated."

I lifted a shoulder and dropped it. "Everything has been a change since my tower."

Zane nodded once more, his ponytail bobbing up and down with the motion. "I cannot express how deeply sorry I feel for any discomfort you may have felt on our part. As you've noticed, our world isn't exactly easy to navigate for mages, let alone humans."

I twisted my hand through my hair and winced, forgetting for a moment about my cut.

"What happened?" Zane held out his hand for me to show him.

I slowly placed my injured hand in his larger one. Zane's fingers were so much longer and thinner than Adam's, his touch just shy of too gentle as if he were the wind brushing against my skin rather than a solid being.

"There was an accident in the kitchen," I explained, leaving out the embarrassing details.

Zane's brows furrowed as he unfurled the cloth Adam had wrapped my finger in. "You really should have Luke heal this. It wouldn't do for it to get infected."

I tugged on my lower lip with my teeth. "Adam said you could help me."

Zane's gaze lifted and fixed on mine. His eyes seemed to be searching for something in my face. If he found it, he didn't give any indication. He also didn't ask me why I didn't want Luke to heal it, for which I was grateful.

"Come along then," he released my hand and sat the watering can down on a nearby stone bench. He led me through the front of the chapel, where the sigil of the mages sat at the front of the room carved into a stone cross. For a moment, rage flared up inside of me, and I had to catch my breath from the force of it.

"Eva?" Zane called to me, pausing by a side door. "Are you alright?"

I sucked in a deep breath and shoved the feelings down. Deep down, where I hoped they would suffocate beneath my lungs. Swallowing thickly, I nodded. "Fine. Just hit my finger."

Accepting my explanation, Zane held the door made of a shiny material open for me.

Stepping into what clearly was his office, my gaze wandered around. There were shelves on every wall, books, and scrolls shoved haphazardly into them. Unlike Adam's desk, which was neat and organized, Zane had just as many books, if not more than on his shelves, stacked on top of it. A part of me wondered how he even got anything done on it.

"Here," Zane shifted a pile of books from a chair in front of his desk and sat it on the floor. Offering me an apologetic smile, he motioned for me to relax. "I don't get many guests back here."

I slid into the chair, my eyes still taking in everything around me. "It's alright. I can see why you wouldn't."

Zane's face flushed, and he pushed his glasses up his nose. "Yes, well, I like to keep busy. It keeps..." he trailed off, and I finished for him.

"Keeps your demon at bay?"

His gaze grew somber. "Yes." After a long moment, he shook himself from his thoughts and knelt before me. "Now, let's see about fixing you up. I must apologize in advance. This isn't my line of study, so there may be some discomfort during the healing process. Luke could probably-"

"It's fine." I interrupted him with an encouraging smile. "I'm tougher than I look."

Zane paused for a moment staring into my eyes. I forced myself to not shift or flinch away from his soul-searching gaze, letting him look all he wanted.

As if speaking more to himself than to me, Zane murmured, "Yes, yes, you are."

He took my hand in his cool ones, unwrapping the cloth from my finger once more. He traced along the cut for a moment and then muttered an incantation under his breath. The skin around the wound warmed until I gasped in pain. My eyes watered as the skin knitted itself back together, and the burning feeling dissipated.

"My apologies." Zane held a handkerchief out to me with a small smile.

"Thank you," I took the handkerchief and rapped at the corners of my eyes before holding it back out to him.

He held his hand up. "Keep it. You may need it again."

I nodded and glanced down at the square white cloth. In one corner, there was writing stitched into it with blood-red thread. ZB, Zane Bishop.

"My mother made that for me," Zane offered the information offhandedly from behind his desk. I hadn't even noticed him move.

"It's nice. The stitching is practically perfect. My stitches always ended up lopsided and loose. My mother always told me that I had better be happy I was pretty, or no man would marry a woman with such sloppy stitching." I laughed, my eyes crinkling at the memory.

Memory.

My eyes widened as they snapped to Zane.

I could only imagine his expression matched mine in shock and delight. I'd had many dreams, but I hadn't had any real memories. Things that I just knew. It relieved me more than I could say to actually know something about myself. Something that wasn't terrifying or just downright confusing.

Zane shuffled through the things on his desk, searching for something. Picking up a little brown book, he flipped the pages quickly and pulled a writing utensil out of his hair, making his red locks cascade around his shoulders.

As he bent his head over the book scribbling something down, his hair fell over his eyes, and he kept having to push it back.

It made me smile. I knew just how Zane felt. My own long locks were a constant hazard, and I was happy to have them above my waistline for once.

Zane's gaze lifted from his book. When he looked at my face, his lips curled at the edges. "What is it? Do I have something on my face?"

I giggled as he touched his cheek.

"You know Adam keeps telling me to stop using these old ink pens." He held up the black utensil in his hand and peered at it thoughtfully. "They aren't practical with the ink being a rare commodity, but I just don't find the modern pens to be the same. You can never get the words to write the way you want." He mimicked writing in the air. "They make everyone's handwriting uniform into serif print." He scoffed. "Serif. The mage who decided that should be the world's font should be dismantled and tossed into the Niagara Pits."

I couldn't help but giggle at him as his nose scrunched up in distaste. I covered my mouth with my hand, trying to stifle the sound, but it just wouldn't stop.

Zane shook his head at me, smiling from ear to ear. "You have a lovely laugh. I wish we had more laughter in this house."

The sadness in his tone made my giggling cut off short.

"Oh, I didn't mean to make you stop." Zane hurried to correct me, shaking his free hand in front of him. "I just meant..." he sighed. "Since the Arch Mage announced his retirement, our house has been on edge. Adam would normally be the next in line to take his grandfather's place, but now Master Tuck has thrown his hat into the ring, so to speak, making everything ten times worse."

I leaned forward in my seat. "Why is everyone so against Master Tuck anyway? I know he doesn't care for humans, so that would be an obvious reason to keep him from taking over. Still, other than that, he seems about the same as the other mages on the council."

Zane shifted back in his seat, lacing his fingers over his chest. "Master Tuck is too much like the others. Which is the problem. We need someone with diversity on the council to keep us mages humble. Master Tuck has long been known for his extreme ways, but he never had much interest in politics until recently." Zane murmured the last bit to himself, deep in thought.

I shrugged. "I have no use for politics. From what you've all told me, I'm to clean and cook and keep thoughts and opinions out of my head that doesn't have to do with either of those." I tried to keep my annoyance out of my voice, but apparently, I hadn't done a decent job of it because Zane frowned.

"I won't apologize again because I'm sure you will get nothing but apologies from the others." He paused. "Maybe not Gage, but the rest of us feel practically sick over it. Forcing you to wait on us goes against everything we believe in."

"Then why do it?" I snipped, standing to my feet. "If you feel so against it."

Zane sighed and removed his glasses, rubbing his face. "All I can say is, those politics you don't care for. Many of us have had to do things we do not wish to even discuss. This is only one of a long list of evils for the greater good." He replaced his glasses and peered up at me, his gaze begging for me to understand.

I gripped my newly healed hand to my chest and jerked my head in a nod. "Thank you for your help. Let me know if there is anything I can assist you with."

Zane pushed his chair back and started toward me, but I'd already moved to the door. I didn't want to hear any more of his excuses or apologies. I didn't care if they were playing a long game. All I knew was the ones I thought were going to be my saviors had changed sides on me, leaving me as just a pawn in their game.

Chapter 5

BY THE TIME I got back to the kitchen, Adam had already finished breakfast. There was a plate waiting for me, but none of the others were around. There were only a few quiches left on the counter, so clearly someone had come to eat. Why they hadn't stayed in the kitchen to eat...

A quick peek in the dining room showed they weren't there either.

Were they avoiding me?

I slid onto a nearby stool, placing my plate in front of me. I found a fork sitting on the counter and grabbed it. Eying the small muffin-shaped mixture, I took a hesitant bite.

"Hmm." At least it tasted good, even if the texture was a bit strange.

Looking around the empty kitchen, I wished one of the others was there to share my opinion on the matter.

Sighing heavily, I leaned my face on my hand and pushed the egg around on my plate.

I wouldn't blame the others for avoiding me. They seemed so conflicted by everything, and while at the start of today I had been so furious with them, I found myself wishing I could help them.

Did I really think so highly of myself that I couldn't cook and clean for them? They had rescued me, and it wasn't like I had anything else to do until I figured out exactly what and who I was.

Which was something else altogether. The more I remembered, the less I wanted to know.

I stabbed the quiche on my plate with my fork.

There had to be more to it than this. I couldn't have been that bad. How could I go from a sweet little girl who loved her mother to someone who could deserve to be locked in a tower the way I had? I needed to figure out who I was and why that person kept trying to come out now.

"Hey, Eva," Luke peeked his head into the kitchen, a hopeful expression on his face.

I sat my fork down and turned in my seat. "Lucas."

His smile dipped a bit at my greeting, but then he sucked in a breath and pushed his shoulders back, getting his wind back for whatever it was he planned to say to me. I wanted to leave the room. I didn't want to give him a chance to apologize to me again. Let alone an opportunity for the other Eva to attack him.

But Zane was right.

I couldn't just keep avoiding him. They had clearly shown they were sorry. I couldn't keep punishing him for it.

"Look," Luke began sliding into the seat next to me, his white cloak billowing out around the chair. "I know you blame me. Hell, I blame me." He shook his head and scoffed in disgust. "I should have said something. Done something. But the mage council, they could take everything from me if I stood up to them." His gaze darkened as he stared down at his hands. "I couldn't bear it if something had happened to you because of me."

I placed my hand on top of his and gave it a small squeeze.

Luke's gaze shifted up to mine.

I offered a smile. "It's alright. I understand. The others already sort of explained it to me." Luke's face brightened, and it made my heart swell with joy. My lips twisted to the side as I continued, "I don't like it, but I don't have much of a choice." I waved my free hand around the room. "Where would I go? I don't know anything about this world or where I would fit into it besides right here." I squeezed his hand once more. "With you."

Luke sat his other hand on top of mine and brought it up between us. "You don't know how happy that makes me." His lips skimmed the edges of our fingertips, and a small thrill went through me where we touched. "And I promise you, we will find a way to get you out of this. We just have to pretend a little longer."

I swallowed hard and nodded.

"So..." Luke lowered our hands but didn't release mine. "What have you learned so far?"

My mouth ticked up at the edges. "I learned that knives are sharp."

"Oh yeah, Adam told me about that." Luke picked up my newly healed hand and critiqued the job Zane had done. "I wish you would have come to me. I'd have taken care of you."

I clasped his hand tightly. "I know. I will next time."

"So that's all you learned? Knives are sharp?" Luke quirked a brow at me, his eyes laughing.

I grinned and ducked my head. "Well, I can clean and cut peppers now, but that's about it. Adam took over after I got hurt."

Smacking the counter with a loud thwack, Luke jumped to his feet and grabbed my hand, dragging me out of my seat as he said, "We can't have that, now can we? What would the other mages think of us? A human who couldn't cook?"

Giggling at his goofy expression, I let him walk me through the cooking process of setting up lunch. Luke taught me to make something simple. Or what he called simple.

Finger sandwiches did not involve actual fingers or being shaped as such as I initially thought. By the end of it, we were both giggling and bumping shoulders with one another. It almost felt like I belonged.

"What's going on here?"

I jerked at Gage's booming voice, causing the plate in my hands to dip and all the tiny sandwiches to fall apart on the floor.

"Jeez, Gage." Luke waved a hand, and the sandwiches put themselves back together on the plate. "Don't be such a dick."

Gage glowered at us from the doorway, his massive biceps bulging as he tightened his folded arms. The tattoo of a dragon wrapped around his arm almost seemed to be moving the way he tensed up. "We are not here to make her life easier. She is to serve us. Not play."

Anger welled up inside of me. I could feel the other Eva pushing at my mind, my fingers itching to wrap around Gage's thick neck and squeeze the prejudiced life out of him. If only I could just-

"Screw you, Gage." Luke stepped between us, blocking my view of the mage, and cutting my anger off at the source. "You know we don't believe in all that crap. Just

because we have to pretend she works for us doesn't mean we have to treat her like garbage."

Gage glided across the room, so silently, I didn't realize he'd moved until his shadow poured over Luke's form. "Watch your tongue. We are being watched all the time. You don't want to give the council a reason to get rid of us as well as *her.*" His eyes shifted over Luke's head so he could glare down at me.

"Actually," Zane's voice interrupted our spat.

Desperate to think of anything but the words coming out of Gage's mouth, I shifted to see Zane in the doorway. He had his tablet in his hand, and his eyes were scanning the screen, his finger tapping it every few moments.

"I finally finished checking the wards, and there are no bugs or spying spells implemented at this time. So, if anyone is watching us, they aren't doing it magically." He smiled at me, making his eyes crinkle behind his glasses.

"You heard him," Luke countered Gage with a fearsome look of his own. "So, back off!"

Gage shot me a final warning look before stalking from the room.

I swallowed down the words the other Eva wanted me to shout at him. It was getting harder and harder to control her, and the fact that I was even able to push her back right now was a miracle. I hated to know what would have happened had Luke not been here.

I sagged until I was practically on the floor from my relief. Luke was far braver than me. Especially since Gage had a good foot of height on him. The sentinel still intimidated me just from being in the same room.

"Are you okay?" Luke placed a hand on my shoulder, and I shifted to him, nodding. "Don't let what he said get to you. He really doesn't believe all that nonsense the council spouts. Gage is just really cautious."

I offered him a weak smile, but it was hard to believe him. I'd never felt so unwelcome as I had with Gage just now. The other Eva really wanted to let him have it, and I couldn't have that.

I wrapped my arms around myself, resisting the urge to shudder.

While I didn't agree with the others about their plan, I didn't want to take my chances out there in a human-hating world, even if I did have my own magic.

"Come on, let's eat!" Luke nudged me in the back to get me moving.

Zane sat at the island with us, reaching for one of the rescued finger sandwiches. "These look great. You did a great job, Eva." He grinned at me as he took a bite.

I ducked my head, my cheeks warming. "It's nothing. Luke did most of it."

Luke bumped my arm. "Don't be so modest. I just told you how to make it. You did the rest."

As we ate our lunch, Zane explained about the monitoring system he had in place for tracking what spells and charms were used around the house. It was all incredibly involved, and I barely understood half of it. Still, I smiled and nodded. Seeing Zane so enthusiastic about something was nice. Better than the other times where he was brooding about the demon inside of him.

Zane's infliction made me wonder if I could talk to him about the other Eva. She was sort of like a demon possession, right? I didn't want her there, and yet she kept rearing her ugly head, making a mess out of my already complicated existence. He would understand what I was going through. He had to. I couldn't keep this to myself much longer. Someone was going to get hurt, and the odds were against the mages who'd rescued me.

"Eva?" Zane stopped what he was doing on his tablet and gave me a curious frown. "Are you alright?"

I nodded vigorously, plastering a smile on my face. "Yes. Of course. What were you saying about the security system?"

Not entirely believing me, he arched a brow and surveyed me for a moment. Then thinking better of it, he leaned forward and showed me his screen. Little lines of shining light interlocked into a sort of weave.

"See these holes?" Zane pointed to the small openings between each line. "That is how tight you want the security in your spell to be. Normally, we wouldn't be too worried about someone trying to sneak anything into our home, but with the council and Master Tuck far too interested in our comings and goings..." Zane slid his finger along a line on the side of the screen. Instantly, the lines moved closer together, and the holes closed.

My brow furrowed. "If it is that simple, why don't you keep your security that tight all the time?"

Luke held a hand out in front of me, his hand glowing faintly. "Because the security is tied to our magic. It takes power to keep it going, and while we'd love to have our security that tight all the time," he chuckled and then lowered his hand, the glow disappearing. "We just aren't that powerful."

"Oh."

I hated to see them having to cripple themselves just to keep me safe. It made me feel like an even more significant burden than I already felt.

Zane sighed and turned the screen dark. "That's enough magic lesson for today. How about something a little easier?"

I arched a brow at him. "What did you have in mind?"

Smiling softly, Zane slipped from his stool and held a hand out to me. "I think you can handle a bit of plant watering, don't you? It's certainly easier than feeding this bottomless pit." He gestured a hand at Luke, who gasped in mock horror.

"I am not a bottomless pit."

Giggling at Luke's antics, I slid my hand into Zane's and allowed him to lead me out of the room. If this was what the rest of the week was going to look like, I couldn't complain. It was certainly better than sitting up in my tower.

Chapter 6

I STARED AT THE black and white contraption, my hand on what I thought was the handle. Today, I was supposed to clean the floors in the hallway. An easy task supposedly, but the machine Adam told me would make the job a quick one bewildered me.

"Go," I commanded the device, giving it a little shake. "Clean," I tried again, frowning hard. I moved my hand along the handle of it, searching for a way to make it go.

The round bottom had brushes all around the base, which I guessed meant it was supposed to scrub the floors. However, it was almost impossible to push it. It was a lot heavier than it looked.

Determined to figure this out without having one of the others come help me, I stepped back from it, crossing my arms as I thought.

Did I need magic to start it? Everything else in this house practically had to have magic poured into it to get it to work. Why should this be any different?

Except it was meant for a human to use.

I was a human.

Or at least, sometimes.

I tugged on the ends of my hair and chewed on my lower lip. Eva, the other Eva, had magic. I knew that for sure. If only I knew how to tap into it on my own.

Closing my eyes, I tried to search myself for the magic I felt before. Still, no matter how much I looked, I didn't find anything. It was just me.

Curling my fingers into fists, I dropped my arms and stomped my foot. This couldn't be that hard! The mages used magic so involuntarily it was as natural as breathing. Why couldn't I do that?

I tried to think of the other times I'd felt the magic inside of me. The first time had been with Zane when his demon had gotten out of control. Then, I'd just done it. I hadn't even known what I was doing until it was already done.

More recently, the times I had felt the magic inside of me had been when the other Eva tried to take over. I didn't have to wonder what set her off. It was easy to decipher that any time I became angry at a mage, she would surface, and the magic would awaken.

That couldn't be too hard. I could get myself mad.

What made me mad?

Being stuck in this time period without my memories. Humans getting treated like less than nothing. The mages acting all superior as if they were gods who could not fall from their pedestals.

Master Tuck's fake smile.

Rebecca's gorgeous face and body plastered all over Adam.

My fists tightened at the thought.

What did Adam even see in her? If she were back in my time, she'd be a street harlot, and Adam wouldn't give her two looks. I'd be the one he praised and caressed.

The one he would kiss and call his one and only.

I shook my head, that wasn't making me mad, only sad.

Alright. Let's try this again.

Gage's idiotic glaring face.

Yes. That's it!

Luke treating me like I was a helpless doll. Blake not giving me more than two-word responses. The way Adam had been so quick to decide I wasn't worth it. Zane's demon calling me evil.

Oooh, that did the trick.

My fingers tingled, and a pressure built up inside my chest almost like I needed to belch.

I found my power, but now how did I use it?

Dropping my gaze to the contraption before me, I lifted my arm. I was just about to try and pour the power into the device when a growling voice stopped me.

"What are you doing?"

My arm jerked back to my side as I spun on my heel. Gage stood in the doorway of the hallway, his brows furrowed, and his lips pressed into a thin line.

When I didn't answer right away, his large boots stomped across the floor until he stopped before me. "I asked you a question."

Opening and shutting my mouth like a gaping fish, I struggled for an explanation. I pointed to the device and then made a sound that even I couldn't decipher as an actual word.

Gage stared at me for a long moment before moving to the black and white device. "You have to turn it on first. Why didn't Adam show you?"

I shrugged, helplessly, not knowing what to say.

His hand grasped the handle, and his thumb stroked down the top of the front of it. A red light flashed, and then a humming began. The brushes on the bottom spun around and around, jerking in Gage's hand as it desperately tried to get away.

Watching Gage, a wicked thought occurred to me. He'd given me nothing but hell since I'd been here. A little revenge might be in order.

Opening my eyes as wide as they could go, I stared at the sentinel blankly. "Now, what do I do?"

Gage looked up from the machine, and his frown deepened. "What do you mean? You just clean the floors." He tried to shove the handle in my direction, but I pretended not to know I was supposed to grab it. The machine spun wildly in place, its grip swinging through the air.

"By the Necronite, what the hell is wrong with you, woman?" Gage growled, trying, and failing to grab the handle as it twisted around at a rhythmic speed. "You're supposed to take the handle."

I shrugged apologetically. "You should have said so. How was I supposed to know? It's not like I've ever used one of these things before."

Jaw clenching, Gage finally snatched the handle of the machine. He moved in close to me. Involuntary, I inhaled, taking in the sweet smell of citrus and pine.

"Here." He grabbed my hand and wrapped my fingers around the handle. Then he waved toward the hallway. "Now clean."

Unable to leave it at that, I blinked dumbly down at the machine and then the hall.

When he noticed I wasn't moving, Gage dragged a hand over his face in exasperation before grabbing the handle from me.

His caramel-colored eyes met mine as he positioned the machine. "You step on the base. Like this." He stepped onto the circular base of it, planting his feet on either side of the handle. "You want to be sure to stand just so, or you'll lose control."

"How?" I pushed even further. "In the middle?"

Gage shot me a glare. "No. Don't put your feet like this." He shifted his feet closer together until they were lined next to each other. "Or you'll lose-"

The machine darted forward and raced down the hallway. I covered my mouth with my hand, hiding my smile.

Gage finally got the machine to stop running down the hallway, but now it kept spinning in circles. The utter frustration on his face was just too much.

Laughing until my sides hurt and I had to lean against the wall to brace myself, I barely noticed when Blake appeared beside me.

"What's going on here?"

I gasped as I tried to stop my laughter, pushing up off the wall to point at Gage.

"Tried to...show me...how...it works..." My laughter couldn't be contained anymore.

Blake rolled his eyes at me and clicked his fingers. The machine stopped abruptly, sending Gage over the handlebars and onto the ground.

This only made me laugh harder.

"What's the problem?" Adam came into the hallway, his red book in his hand, as he peered at the scene. A hint of a smile tipped his lips, but he quickly squashed it as Gage stomped over to us.

"Why didn't you teach her to use the buffer?" Gage glowered in my direction before turning his annoyance back on Adam.

Adam pursed his lips, his brow drawing downward. "I did tell Eva how to use it. I just forgot to tell her how to turn it on. That's what I came back for." His mouth quirked up on one side. "But it seems like you already helped her out."

If looks could kill, I'd be buried right then and there.

Gage gritted his teeth and bit out, "Why did you act like you didn't know how to use it then?"

I shrugged and forced my face to be serious. "I didn't know how to use it, I only know what Adam told me. I'd never used it before. So, it only made sense to have someone who had to show me. Don't you think?"

Adam and even Blake chuckled a little at that until Gage shot them a murderous scowl.

Clearing his throat, Adam pointed his book at Gage. "She's right, you know. A demonstration was in order. Thank you for stepping up, friend."

Gage stared at us for a long second before he huffed and pushed past us stomping down the hall.

I winced as a door slammed somewhere in the distance. "Do you think he's mad?"

Blake arched a brow. "Let's just say I wouldn't want to be you right now."

My shoulders bunched up at my neck, and I pouted. "It's not my fault he doesn't have a sense of humor."

Adam placed a hand on my shoulder. "Don't worry about it. He'll get over it."

Blake snorted and muttered, "After he has his revenge."

I startled. "Wha...what? What revenge?"

"You embarrassed him," Blake explained, waving an arm down the hallway. "And that is not a mage who is easily embarrassed. Repercussions are sure to follow."

I hadn't thought of that. I wanted to get back at Gage for being so rude to me all the time, but I didn't know he'd want to get me back for my retaliation.

"No use in stressing over it." Adam lowered his hand to my back and gave me a little push forward. "Let's go work on dinner. I think you're ready for something a little more complicated, don't you?"

I forced a smile to my face, though my insides were tightening up until I felt like they were eating themselves. The penalty for my actions hadn't ever come to my mind. I'd thought Gage would just figure I was being a silly human and leave it at that. He probably would have had Adam not come and blown it all.

I sighed to myself, earning me a strange look from Adam.

I suppose I just wasn't cut out for villainous plots after all.

Chapter 7

A BELL CHIMED THROUGHOUT the house as I finished putting a plate of bread on the dining room table. Wiping my hands on the apron Adam had given me, I frowned at the sound. "What was that?"

"Someone's at the door," Blake grumbled as he plopped into his chair. Without waiting for me and the others, he began to fill his plate up.

I briefly wondered who could be at the door on my way back to the kitchen.

"You're supposed to answer it."

Pausing in the doorway of the kitchen, I turned back to him. "Why?"

Shrugging a shoulder as he began shoving greens into his mouth, the bell chimed again and again. Someone was getting impatient.

Sighing because I obviously wasn't going to get an answer from the darker head twin, I made my way to the front of the house. On the way, Izzy danced and yipped in the hallway, almost knocking me off my feet.

Giggling, I stepped over her and shook my head. "Izzy, you silly hellhound. Go find your master. Go on." I shooed her toward the dining room, where Blake would no doubt feed her from his plate.

Zane rounded the corner of the hallway just as I was getting to the door and whispered, "Who is it?"

I glanced his way and lifted my hands. "I don't know. I haven't answered it yet. Which by the way, I have a question about."

Staring at the door for a moment, I realized I'd never had to answer the door before. I wasn't even sure how to open the thing. It usually opened for me automatically.

Zane reached over me and pointed to the side of the door. "Push that button there."

I pushed the button on the side of the door as instructed. A light shot out, and a small translucent image of Master Tuck appeared. "Master Tuck?"

"Oh, good. Eva." The miniature version of himself turned to Zane as well. "And Cleric Zane. I have come to check on Eva's progress. I have a notice here from the council giving me permission to drop by unannounced."

Zane frowned but didn't protest. Not that he needed to. I already knew how they felt about Master Tuck. Having him show up whenever he felt like it wasn't going to be suitable for any of us.

"I programmed the door to your face," Zane explained out of the blue, and I blinked at him. Placing a hand on my shoulder, he gave me a little nudge to move over. "Look right here." He pointed to a small black box that once I was in position, lit up. A line of light slid over my face making me squint against the brightness.

"Eva. Access granted," a monotone voice announced from the wall. Then, the door slid open revealing Master Tuck.

"Ah, there we are." Master Tuck fluffed his robes around his pudgy middle and glanced between the two of us. "It is nice to see you, Cleric Zane. And you, Eva. How are you getting along?"

I inclined my head, not sure how to respond.

"We were just sitting down to dinner," Zane explained. I envied how he was able to keep a pleasant tone in his voice without giving away how the other mage made him really feel. "Would you like to join us? Eva made it."

Master Tuck glanced at me with a delighted, if not surprised expression. "Did she now? Then how could I possibly refuse."

Zane led Master Tuck down the hallway, and without being told, I trailed behind him imitating the other humans outside of the house. The others hadn't made me walk behind them yet, but if Master Tuck was here to check up on me, then I was sure he expected it.

When we arrived at the dining room, all but Gage had taken their seats. I walked as quickly as I could toward the kitchen while Master Tuck made his greetings to the room.

While I was gathering up the last dish to take to the table, Adam came into the kitchen, a forced smile on his face.

"Eva." He stopped me from entering the room, his face the picture of distress. "Master Tuck is here."

"Yes, I see that." I inclined my head to the dining room and tried to pass by him, but he blocked my path. "This isn't light, Adam."

"What I mean is...that...ugh." Adam dragged a hand over his face and jerked the silver strands on his head. "Tuck's going to want you to act like a real human."

I shifted the weight of the plate in my arms. "I am a real human, Adam."

"I mean, you have to serve us, each of us, at the table," Adam winced as he awkwardly explained what he meant.

"Okay?" I cocked my head to the side. "I can do that."

"But...now don't get mad," he held his hands up in front of him, trying to ward off an attack that I had no intention of making. "You can't speak to us unless spoken to, and you have to keep your eyes down."

My eyes narrowed, and I could feel the itching at the back of my mind. Taking a deep breath, I forced myself to keep calm though I wanted to throw the very plate in my hands on Master Tuck's head. With a long-exasperated sigh I said, "Fine."

Adam's tense form visibly relaxed. "Fine? Really?"

"Yes," I clipped, getting tired of his delaying. "Can I get this over with now?"

Adam nodded and shifted to the side, letting me pass.

Acutely aware of the eyes on me as I walked into the dining room, I kept my eyes down on the plate in my hands. If this was what it took to get the prejudiced old man out of the house, then I would be the best god damn servant I could be. Starting at Luke, I scooped from the plate of a noodle and sauce mixture Adam had spent all afternoon helping me make.

I was actually quite proud of what I'd been able to learn. In another place, another time, where I wasn't pretending to be their lowly servant, I might have actually enjoyed cooking for the men in the house. There was something about creating things with my hands that I really enjoyed.

Standing so close to Adam hadn't been bad either. Though, he had made sure that what happened last time didn't repeat itself.

He kept his hands to himself but just having him so close to me was rough. His presence there as we worked, talked, and laughed together, had been torture. Thankfully, I was so tense over his nearness that the other Eva had no chance of coming forth. Now, though, I could feel her already, just below the surface. I needed to get this done with and get out of here before someone got hurt.

"I am so surprised by Eva's progress," Master Tuck mused as I made my way around his side of the table. "Just a few days ago, she was this willful human doing whatever she willed, and here's Eva now, a perfect picture of a subservient human, right where she belongs."

My jaw tightened, and the vein in my head pulsed.

No. No. Not now.

Adam chuckled, drawing my attention. "Yes. We were surprised ourselves at how easy it was to tame our Eva."

"I'm done, Eva." Luke held his plate out to me with an apologetic puppy dog face, wilting my anger a tiny bit.

I took his plate and utensils and dipped my head, not sure how I was allowed to respond.

"Well, you have done very well, Master Adam. I can see why your grandfather would back you for Arch Mage." Master Tuck drank deeply from his cup, his eyes peering over the rim with a suspicious twinkle in them.

Adam glanced up at me as I passed by, grabbing my elbow to stop me. "Hold on a moment, Eva. Master Tuck is giving you a compliment. You should be here for this."

I gritted my teeth together and stared hard down at the plate in my hands.

"I was just telling, Master Adam here, how well you are doing. You're cooking and serving meals already?" He took a bite of his food and hummed in delight. "And it's so good! My girl isn't half as good as this, and she's been working for us for years. You must have a natural talent for cooking." He laughed and shoved another forkful into his mouth.

"Thank you, Master Tuck." I pushed my mouth into a smile, though, from the choking laugh that came from Luke, it wasn't a nice one.

"It was a little touch and go for a bit there. We had an accident the first time, and this meal almost didn't happen." Adam took a large bite of his food, and I wished with all my might that he would choke on it. Unfortunately, he didn't and swallowed to only keep talking. "Eva didn't know that you had to keep mixing the meat or it would burn. She'd already left the room before I realized she didn't know." He chortled as he patted my arm repeatedly.

I went to the bathroom. How was I supposed to know I had to keep watching the meat? It was all Adam's fault. He's the one who left me unsupervised to go answer a call.

"Though, I did leave her alone to take a call," Adam smirked and lifted his glass toward the hallway. "That was a mistake."

From the corner of my eye, I saw Blake shake his head, covering his good eye with his hand.

"That's true." Master Tuck laughed so hard his belly jiggled. My fingers tightened on the plate. "New human workers are hard to break in. Usually, you have a veteran servant train them. I commend you a lot for taking on the responsibility yourself. It must be quite a handful to do your normal work as well as teaching Eva how to do all of hers."

Red filled my vision.

"Ah, no. Not Eva." Adam leaned back in his chair to give me what I suspected he thought was an encouraging nod, but it only made me want to smash the plate in my hands over his head. "No, our girl here, is a natural. Why, you wouldn't even know she spent a thousand years in a tower? Eva basically has to relearn everything, and I don't mean to ring my own gong, but-" Adam let out a high-pitched yowl, his eyes bugged out of his head as his mouth formed a pained expression.

Everyone was staring at me, and I wanted to ask what they were all looking at when my eyes dropped to the table.

I gasped and jumped back, my hands going to my mouth in horror.

The fork that'd been on Luke's place now stood straight up in Adam's hand.

"Eva, what in the-" Adam began, but Master Tuck cut in.

"That woman is a menace." He pushed from his chair, his nostrils flaring. "She's not ready to be out in the real world. In fact, I'm not even sure she should stay here with you any longer."

"Oh, my God." I shook my head, my eyes burning with tears. "What have I done?"

"Eva, it's alright." Luke shoved his chair away and moved toward us. "I can heal Adam. Don't cry."

I shook my head and backed away from him. "No. It's not okay."

"Exactly!" Master Tuck moved at me, reaching out to grab me. "There are laws against harming mages, human. They'll have you locked up!"

I stumbled back from him, wrapping my arms around my middle. I didn't trust anyone to touch me right now. I didn't even trust myself.

This was too much.

"That's not your decision to make." Zane stood so fast his chair fell over. "I think you should leave. We can handle this, Master Tuck."

"Now, see here." Master Tuck gave me his back to argue with Zane.

Taking the moment of distraction, I inched toward the door. Luke started fussing over Adam's hand, taking in the damage. Blake sat quietly in his seat, watching the whole interaction with intense speculation. I was only thankful that Gage hadn't shown his face yet.

When I reached the door, I pivoted on my heel and took off down the hallway. Luke called out to me once more, but I didn't stop until I pushed my way through the double doors of the chapel.

My heart pounded in my chest so hard I felt it might fly right out of it. I stared down at my hands in utter horror as I paced the chapel floor.

What had I done?

When had I done it? I didn't even remember grabbing the fork, let alone stabbing it into Adam's hand!

This was getting ridiculous. How could I trust myself around anyone if I couldn't even control my body? At this rate, the other Eva was going to take me over completely, and I didn't know how to stop it.

Tears streaming down my face, I cried into the empty room, "What do you want from me? Why do you keep doing this?"

But I received no answer.

Figures.

The only time she deemed herself worthy of showing was when she wanted to cause chaos in my life.

I sank down onto a nearby bench and laid my head in my hands.

Damn her and damn the mages for saving me from that accursed tower.

Chapter 8

I WASN'T SURE HOW long I cried and wallowed in my despair before a soft hand touched my back. I jerked away from it, scrambling off the bench and onto my feet as I wrapped my arms around myself.

"It's alright, Eva. It's just me." Zane held his hands up.

I shook my head, shoving the hair that had plastered to my tears off my face. "Stay away. It's not safe."

Zane lowered his hands but didn't come toward me. Leaning his elbows on his knees, he peered at me patiently. "No one's mad at you. Adam's fine. Luke healed him right up." He offered me a hopeful smile, but I only gripped my shoulders tighter.

"You should never have saved me. The council was right." I spun away from him, my tears welling up once more. "I deserved to be in that tower. She deserves it."

"Who does?"

I paused for a moment then took a deep breath, dropping my arms as I turned back to Zane. "The other Eva. The queen. Or at least, I think that's what I was."

Zane's head tilted slightly as he took in my words. "And this queen. Do you know who she was?"

I shook my head and then stopped. "Yes. Actually. Maybe." I took a step closer to him, my hands wringing in front of me. "I keep having dreams. Memories. I think. One of the first ones I had here..." I trailed off, not sure if I should tell him.

"Go on."

Sighing heavily, I squatted down on the ground, wrapping my arms around my knees. "I dreamed I was getting married...to King Midas."

Zane didn't say anything for a long moment. I stared hard at the stone floor, not wanting to see the expression on his face.

"Well, at least, we have a starting point on where to look for information about you."

My head jerked up. I met Zane's gaze, those hazel orbs so carefully neutral, not giving me any idea of how he really felt.

"But that doesn't explain why you suddenly attacked Adam?" Zane pushed his glasses up his nose as he leveled a look at me. "And Luke mentioned a similar peculiar incident with him."

I sank to the floor completely, hanging my head down. "The more I remember, the more memories I obtain, the more I can feel her."

"Feel her?"

I tapped the side of my head. "In here and..." I gripped the dress over my heart. "...in here." My eyes burned as I looked up at Zane. "She's so angry, Zane. I've never felt something so fierce. It feels like I'm burning up from the inside when she comes, and I don't want to hurt you. Any of you."

Zane slid off the bench and crawled on his knees over to me. "It's alright, Eva. We won't let anything happen to you or us. We'll figure this out."

I reached out toward him, my heart aching. "I'm so sorry. I can't...I can't stop her...I keep trying, but I-" Zane wrapped his arms around me, pulling me into a tight embrace. I cried into his chest, my fingers curling into his shirt as I held on tight.

"Shhh," Zane whispered against my hair as he stroked my head. "It'll all be okay. One thing at a time."

"How, though?" I leaned back from him, swiping a hand over my face. "The more time we take, the more likely I'll hurt someone. You should just shove me back into that tower where I can't hurt anyone."

As much as I didn't want to go back, I didn't know what else to do. The thought of hurting one of these men, of hurting anyone, made me sick. Even the mages like Master Tuck with their backward thinking didn't deserve what she wanted to do to them.

She wanted them to suffer. Oh, did she want them to hurt. The way they had hurt her. Even if it meant killing them all.

"First off," Zane began, pulling me from my thoughts. "We need to figure out what triggers her. That's what I had to do with..." he trailed off. Zane angled his head back and closed his eyes, taking a deep breath in before letting it out.

"What?" My fingers tightened in his shirt. "What is it?"

"Nothing," Zane growled a little harsher than before, and I released him abruptly, shifting away.

"Zane?"

Shaking his head, Zane rubbed at his chest. "It's me. I'm alright. It's just..." he huffed a laugh. "Here I am talking about triggers, and I'm sitting right in front of one of mine."

I frowned. "What do you mean?"

"You." Zane sighed and sank onto the ground, leaning against a nearby column. "The demon really seems to like you."

I snorted. "That doesn't seem likely." The sweet Zane was so much different than the demonic being living inside of him only contained by the sigil tattooed into his chest. The demon wanted to hurt me, to hurt Zane. Anything to get back at being imprisoned.

I guess it saw a kinship in me. Something I hadn't let myself think too hard about. That was until the other Eva had started making her appearance. Now I wished I'd listened to what the demon had to say.

Shifting over to Zane, but not touching him, I asked, "What else triggers it?"

Zane lifted his head from the column and looked at me. "Loud crowds. Any physical altercation. It likes chaos. It really likes blood." He paused and turned his gaze to the side. "I haven't been able to be close to anyone since it happened. I'm too afraid of what might happen if I lost control."

I cocked my head to the side, not sure what he meant. His eyes flickered to mine, his cheeks turning pink.

"Oh!" My eyes widened. "Oh. I could see how that could be hard. I don't have any advice I could give." I paused for a moment and pressed my hands to my face as a thought occurred to me. "I don't even know if I've ever had such a closeness with someone else."

"You were married," Zane offered. "In the medieval period. They were pretty strict about consummating a marriage. They had bedding parties and everything." I stared at Zane, appalled at the thought of having an audience for something so private. Zane flushed at my stare and stumbled over his words. "I believe the likelihood would be quite high."

"Yes." I sank back on my heels. "I suppose you're right."

The memory of King Midas came to my mind. I couldn't help the way my face contorted at the thought of making love to such a man. He wasn't unattractive, but still, he wasn't anywhere close to Zane or any of the others. Even Gage.

My cheeks burned as I peered up at Zane beneath my lashes. I couldn't believe what I'd been thinking and right beside him.

Zane's gaze met mine, and for a long moment, we simply stared at one another, neither one of us seeming to want to break the moment.

The chapel doors banged open.

"There you are!" Adam announced.

Zane and I jumped in place, our eyes darting away from each other. Zane pushed off the column and stood, offering me a hand to stand. I shifted to my knees and allowed him to help me up.

Adam stopped before us, his eyes moving between the two of us. "Did I interrupt something?"

"No," Zane and I quickly answered. We met each other's gaze for a moment before I broke it, turning my head to the side and grabbed one elbow with my hand.

"Your hand looks good." Zane stepped closer to Adam, almost as if he were protecting me from him.

I chanced a look at Adam's hand, noticing unbroken skin with eminence relief. No one would ever know I'd stabbed him. The skin was so unblemished.

Adam lifted his hand and smiled. "Yeah. Luke sure has a way with healing. Hardly felt a thing. I mean, after I got the fork out of my hand."

Zane made a sound in the back of his throat and jerked his head in my direction. "We have a situation."

"I'd say." Adam looped his fingers into the belt of his pants and rocked on his heels. "I admit I did get a bit carried away on the ruse with Master Tuck, but I didn't think you'd get so upset about it. I'm sorry if I hurt your feelings." Adam lifted his hand and reached for me.

I stumbled back a few steps. "Please don't. I don't know if she will come back."

Adam frowned, his brows furrowing. He shot a look at Zane. "She? Did someone come when I was being healed?"

Zane touched Adam on the shoulder. "Eva is starting to remember who she was."

"That's great!" Adam smiled at me with far more enthusiasm than I had.

"Unfortunately, it has come with some side effects," Zane continued as if it were just a minor inconvenience that my alter ego wanted to kill them all.

Adam's face contorted in confusion. "What do you mean? Is that why you stabbed me? Is it causing some kind of hormonal fit? Should we go back to the hospital?" Adam stepped toward me, his eyes scanning over me. "Maybe that spell did some lasting damage we don't know about."

Zane grabbed Adam by the elbow, pulling him back and out of my space. "It's not like that. At least, I don't believe so." He paused and glanced over at me for a moment. "It seems that the person Eva was before she went into the tower is trying to emerge, causing certain incidents like at dinner."

Looking thoughtful, Adam flexed his recently healed hand and frowned harder. "Alright. I suppose we'll just have to deal with the new Eva as she comes." Adam's lips quirked up at the edges. "And keep you away from sharp objects."

My lips twitched at his joke, but it was forced down as I remembered what Zane and I had been talking about.

"About the trigger."

"Oh, yes." Zane shifted, putting his hands in his pockets. "We were discussing possible events or people who might incur the queen's wrath."

"Queen's?" Adam arched a brow.

Zane waved him off. "I'll get into it later. In any case, once we know what triggers her, then we can work on controlling her." He peered over the rim of his glasses, scanning me as if the answer were right there. When his eyes settled on my face, he asked, "Any ideas?"

I shrugged, shaking my head slightly, then muttering, "Mages."

"Excuse me?" Zane leaned toward me. "What was that?"

I sighed and dropped my arms. Might as well get it over with. "Mages. She hates the whole lot of you and wants you all to die a fiery torturous death."

Zane and Adam went silent.

When they didn't respond for longer than a minute, I thought I might have broken them. Then finally, Adam turned to Zane with a grin.

"And you thought the election was all we had to worry about this year."

Chapter 9

TO MY RELIEF, ZANE and Adam suggested I call it a night. If Blake and Luke had anything to say about what happened at dinner, they didn't have the chance to confront me.

However, when I woke the next morning, I found a pile of dresses at my door.

More servant uniforms.

I grimaced as I leaned down to pick them up. Except when my fingers touched the natural fabric of the dresses, they weren't rough and itchy like the one I wore. They looked the same, and yet they felt like the smoothest silk.

A tiny smile crept up my face as I went back into my room.

Blake.

As I changed out of my old uniform, I smiled wider. I never thought grumpy Blake would be so considerate.

Still, Izzy liked him, and she was a big sweetheart. That meant he had to have a heart in there somewhere. This act of kindness only proved it.

My fingers slid over the material. I sighed. The material felt like I was being caressed by the softest of feathers. Blake definitely knew how to impress a woman.

Now, if only he could smile once in a while.

Shaking my head at the impossible, I made my way out of my room and up the stairs. When I reached the top of the stairs, I half expected Blake to be there behind the door.

I had to admit I was a little disappointed he wasn't there when I opened the door.

A little nervous about what would happen today, I walked as slow as possible down the hall. We hadn't discussed what had happened in completion. What about Master Tuck? He'd seen what I'd done. Would he report it to the council? Would they be here at any moment to take me away?

The door chimed.

I froze in place.

Were they mind readers as well? No. No. It couldn't be. It's just a coincidence.

Convincing myself it wasn't Master Tuck or the council here to take me away, I forced my feet toward the door. Each jerky movement of my tense body made my pulse race faster.

I swallowed thickly as a shaky hand lifted to push the button Zane had shown me before.

"Hello?" my voice came out a croak as I squinted at the image coming to life. A curvy figure clad in a skintight dress flipped their long hair over their shoulder.

"Oh. It's you," the familiar sultry voice answered upon clearing.

Rebecca. Of course. Just what I needed today.

"Can I help you?" I forced a sickly-sweet tone into my voice as I smiled politely.

Rebecca's lovely face didn't change from her bored expression as she examined her nails. "You can let me in. I have an appointment with Adam."

Pressing my lips into a tight line, I hesitated to open the door. I didn't like this woman. Not because she was gorgeous in a way, I could never be. Or because she used to be Adam's lover. Okay. So, the last one might have a little bit to do with it, but still, there was something about her I didn't trust.

"Well, come on now. Open up."

I lowered my hand from the door. "I apologize, but I will have to check with Master Adam first. You understand?"

"I certainly do not!" Her voice screeched, her hands dropping into fists at her side as she stomped her foot. "Let me in this instant."

I pushed the same button again, and the transparent image of Rebecca disappeared. With a smugness about me, I took my time walking to Adam's office.

While I didn't like being a servant in their house, it did give me a newfound power that I didn't completely hate.

Stopping outside of Adam's office, I contemplated if I had to knock or not. Finally, I just decided to enter without knocking. If Adam wanted me to do differently, he'd tell me.

I found Adam standing over his desk, a pensive look on his handsome face.

When I walked in, his head lifted. The thoughtfulness in his eyes morphed to pleasant surprise, and I couldn't help but preen inside. "Eva. How are you this morning?"

Approaching the desk, I noticed the book he had been worrying over. "Concealment spells?"

Face going blank, Adam closed the book and cleared his throat. "Oh. Yes. I decided to take a deeper look into your tower. Zane is working on finding out what books and scrolls the council might have on King Midas."

I nodded, waiting there, awkwardly.

"I never apologized-"

"Did you want-"

We both stopped talking and laughed.

Adam walked around the side of the desk and leaned back against it, waving a hand at me. "You first."

Feeling shy, I wrung my hands in my skirts. "I was going to say, I'm sorry for stabbing you." I inclined my head toward his hand.

Adam lifted his hand and stared at it for a moment before smiling. "Don't worry about it. Please. It's not like you could control it, right?"

I nodded profusely. "Right."

"Though, it was a struggle to get Master Tuck to leave." I tensed at his words. He chuckled. "Luke and Blake had to convince him it was a muscle spasm as a result of the stasis spell."

My eyes widened. "And he accepted that?"

Adam shook his head. "He seemed to, but I doubt it. We'll probably hear from him soon. Or one of the council members."

Ugh. That reminded me.

"Rebecca is here."

Eyebrows furrowing, Adam straightened. "Rebecca?" He paused and pressed his lips into a tight line. "Oh, yes. I forgot about her."

My stomach sank. "So, you do have an appointment with her?"

Adam gave me a grim smile. "Unfortunately, yes."

"Then, I probably should let her in." I grimaced, imagining the earful I was likely to get from the woman.

Adam sighed and moved toward the door. "No. I'll get it. Go find Zane. He's bound to be back by now. He was supposed to meet with Gage in the library."

I tensed.

Gage hadn't been around since the cleaning incident. Part of me wanted to avoid him even at the cost of missing out on finding more information on myself.

Scrounging up my courage, I walked with my head high out of Adam's office and down the hall toward the library.

A familiar voice shouted, "Izzy! Come back," before a scaly bundle of fur came bounding around the corner.

I had about a second to brace myself before I was knocked off my feet, and a long slimy tongue slid over my face.

"Ugh, Izzy," I giggled and pushed at the hellhound. "Get off."

Izzy yipped and bounced in place, luckily her paws were on either side of me and not right on my chest. A ringed hand appeared above me, wrapping around the collar around her neck.

"Come on, you. Get off her." Blake's face appeared above me as he pulled Izzy off. His one golden eye gave her a chastising look before he offered me a hand. "Sorry. She needs to be walked."

Surprised by his offer, I stared at his hand until he frowned and dropped his hand. "I don't have cooties."

My brow furrowed. "Cooties?"

"Germs. A disease. Whatever you want to call it." Blake stood and backed away.

"Oh." I scrambled gracefully to my feet and brushed my skirt off. Feeling the silkiness of my dress, I reached a hand out to stop Blake from leaving. "Wait. I mean, I wanted to thank you, you know, for my dresses."

Blake bobbed his head, his black hair falling over his face more.

I could barely see the purple of his other eye between the strands of hair. I wondered briefly if he would ever trust me enough to let me look him straight in the eyes.

"Also, about dinner..." I trailed off, lacing my fingers behind my back.

"Don't worry about it. Adam and Zane explained everything," Blake clipped gruffly. "Not your fault."

I cocked my head to the side as I watched him. "So, you don't want to send me away?"

Blake scratched Izzy's head, his gaze down on her. "I know what it's like to be unable to control a part of you. We all do. If we damned you for the very thing that made us different, what would that say about us?"

My chest tightened with emotion. Not wanting to push any further and cause Blake to go back into his shell, I nodded. "Well, I have to get to the library. Zane's waiting for me."

"Gage is in there." Blake looked up from Izzy to meet my gaze, a mischievous twinkle in his eye.

I groaned. "Don't remind me."

"Watch your back."

I stepped forward and trailed my fingers over Izzy. When they skimmed over Blake's, we both froze.

Peering up at him beneath my lashes, I waited to see if he would panic and say something mean like he always did.

To my surprise, Blake took my hand and shifted it beneath one of Izzy's ears.

"She likes it when you scratch her here."

Swallowing hard, my heart skipped as I scratched at Izzy's ear.

The hellhound practically purred her tail, swinging around to smack the ground behind her.

"See?" Blake told me, his voice low, "It turns her into a big pile of mush."

I could relate. From this position, I could just see under his hair right into both eyes. It was an intense experience I hadn't been prepared for. The violet and gold of his eyes zeroed in on me, taking in everything I had and giving nothing in return.

Finding it hard to breathe, I turned my head, breaking the connection as I slid my hand out from under his. "I better go."

"Alright, come on Izzy."

The hurt in his voice made me want to stop him. Yet, I didn't. I let Blake walk away and watched where he'd been long after he left.

Blowing out a long breath, I readied myself for another confrontation. This one at least would be less complicated than this. Gage only wanted one thing from me.

Revenge.

Chapter 10

UNFORTUNATELY, I DIDN'T RUN into anyone else on my way to the library. It was no use to delay the inevitable. I just had to do the honorable thing and face my punishment.

I pushed the library door open.

Zane sat at a table with books and scrolls piled high. His blood-red hair was braided over one shoulder, but it was coming apart.

Groaning, Zane tugged on his braid and then pushed his glasses up his nose though they didn't need to be moved.

Taking a step into the library, I cautiously moved toward Zane. Just because I didn't see Gage didn't mean he wasn't there.

Zane didn't look up from the book he was reading even when I was at his elbow.

"Find anything?"

Head jerking up, Zane's eyes widened, and his shoulders bunched up. After seeing it was me, he relaxed and sighed, tugging on his braid again.

"No. Not yet." He waved a hand at the pile on the table. "These all came today. Every reference of King Midas in the council's archives. If we are going to find anything, it'll be there."

I chose the seat next to him and sank down into it. Glancing around the library, I chewed on my lower lip.

Where was Gage?

Was he waiting in the shadows to jump me?

Did he enjoy making me worry about his attack?

Damn. What was I going to do? I couldn't focus like this. I had to know.

"Gage had to leave for a job."

My eyes swung over to Zane. "What?"

Zane offered me a small smile. "You seemed worried. So, I thought I'd ease your mind. He's going to be gone for a few days."

"Oh." I sagged in my chair far more relieved than I expected. So as to save face, I asked conversationally, "Does he do that often? Leave for several days."

Zane nodded, turning back to his book. "Sure. It's his job. He goes where the council needs him."

Interesting. Then I remembered what Luke had said and tensed. Gage was an assassin. An assassin for the council of mages. And I made him mad!

Good job. Just good work. Not like I didn't have enough to worry about. Now I had to worry about getting killed in the middle of the night. Or maybe poisoned. Poison was easier to get away with, wasn't it?

"Relax, Eva." Zane placed his hand on mine.

"Huh?"

"Remember your trigger. If you get too worked up..."

My eyes widened. "Oh, my God. I hadn't even thought about that." I shook my head and straightened myself out. "You're right. I have to stay in control. Relax." Think about something else. "What do you do for the council?"

"What do you mean?" Zane flipped the page of his book.

"Don't you all work for them?"

Zane made a sound in the back of his throat that sounded like a cross between a snort and a laugh. "They would love that. However, no. I do not work for the council. That's Adam and Gage's thing."

"So, what do you do?" I moved to the edge of my chair, genuinely interested.

Looking away from his book, Zane's eyes squinted at the edges as he smiled at me. "Why this, of course. I research long lost histories. I mainly work with a grant. Money given by the council to do my work. However," he added quickly, "that doesn't mean I work for them. What I do benefits all of us. Helping to keep our histories from repeating themselves." He pushed his glasses up with his middle finger. "Sometimes, I take commissions from other mages to find information on all manner of things. Events. Artifacts. Spells."

I frowned. "So, you're taking time away from your work to find out about me. I'm sorry." I pulled my lower lip between my teeth, worrying it. "I don't have any money to pay you. I suppose I'm already indebted to you all as it is." I gave a small, sad laugh, but Zane simply took my hand in his.

"Do not think for a moment you are hindering me or the others. We want to help you. I like you, Eva. I hope we can be good friends one day." He chuckled slightly. "Once we get your past under control, of course."

I smiled back. "Of course."

Zane released my hand and went back to his book.

Picking up the nearest book, I flipped open to the index. Not really reading anything, I put the book down and asked, "What about Blake and Luke? Do they work for the council?"

Zane gave me a patient smile, placing his book down. "Luke and Blake have their own business. Luke takes on clients for healing. Usually, more complex issues that the hospital cannot handle. Mishaps with magic usually."

"And Blake?"

I tried to make it, so I didn't seem more interested in one of them than the other. But while Luke was so much more forthcoming about himself and his feelings, his twin was still a mystery. Even with the small peeks I'd seen into his walls lately.

Zane's lips twitched. Only slightly. I wouldn't have even seen it had I not been staring at him so intently.

I felt my face redden without meaning to. Choosing to ignore it, thankfully, Zane didn't comment.

"Blake is a conjurer as you know," Zane explained. "He works with other mages to strengthen their spells and other rituals. It requires quite a lot of prep time, which can be quite lonely."

I almost didn't believe I heard the last part, but the amusement in Zane's eyes was apparent.

Did Zane want me to get closer to Blake?

That didn't make sense. If the demon's words were valid. Zane had at least a physical interest, if not a romantic interest in me. Why would he want me to pursue his friend?

"Of course, Luke and Blake are the youngest of us and still have to go through the mage's trials." Zane continued reading once more, keeping his thoughts to himself.

"Oh. What does that entail? Am I allowed to ask that?" I added on in one breath.

Zane chuckled. "It's different for each mage. Usually, they meet with a senior mage of their chosen art, and they test them on everything they should know to be masters of their arts."

"Are you a master? I mean, they don't call you Master like Adam or Tuck."

Shaking his head, Zane stood. He strode to a nearby bookshelf and skimmed the titles. Finding the one he wanted, he pulled it from the shelf and walked back to the table. "Here. This will explain the more complexities of the mage hierarchy. Each art has its own title for a master. I never allowed myself to get stronger than I am because..." he trailed off, and I nodded in understanding.

The demon.

I'd only had a small taste of the magic I had inside of me. Combine that with the rage the other Eva had for the mages, and she could cause a lot of damage. I wouldn't want to give more ammunition to her than I had to. Just as Zane didn't.

"Thank you." I took the book and sat it next to me. I'd look over it when I had free time. Maybe I would find something that would help me control my powers or at least keep them away from her.

Zane bobbed his head and picked his book back up. I glanced back down at the book in front of me and tried to focus on what I was looking for.

Midas. King Midas. Golden hand. Anything to do with those things. I doubted they had put a passage about the other Eva by herself. From what the others had already told me, they didn't know much about the queen, and the golden hand had been nothing more than a legend.

After a while of staring at the books, I stopped to rub my eyes.

"It does strain the eyes, doesn't it?" Zane commented as he sat another scroll aside.

Trailing my fingers through my hair, I gathered it up off my neck. "I don't know how you do it every day. We've only been doing this for..." I searched for one of those clocks they'd shown me.

"An hour."

My eyes widened, and I groaned. "Only an hour? We're never going to get done." I laid my head down on the table with a whimper.

A hand stroked the back of my head, and I hummed in pleasure.

"That's nice."

"We'll find something. If not here, then somewhere else."

That reminded me. I lifted my head abruptly. "I saw Adam this morning."

"Oh?"

"He mentioned he was looking into the tower. What exactly is he looking for?" I didn't know precisely why I asked. For some reason, I was feeling protective of the stack of stone that had been my prison for the last thousand years.

Zane shrugged. "If we can find out who hid the tower, then we might be able to find out who put you there. There weren't many people in this part of the world at the end of the middle ages. Certainly not any colonies then. Not yet, anyway. It definitely narrows down the prospects."

I hummed and then had a thought. "There was a memory I had. A woman." I tried to recall what she looked like.

"Do you remember anything about her?" Zane pulled out the book he had in his office, his pen at the ready. "Her name? Anything?"

"Black hair. Red lips." I stroked my lower lip in thought. "She was some kind of queen. I don't know from where. She said I'd..." I cut myself off, swallowing against the bile rising as I remembered. "That I had..."

"It's alright, Eva." Zane reached out and patted my hand. "That wasn't you. Not anymore."

I nodded jerkily and took a deep breath. "I killed her husband. Quite viciously. And her father. I think." The woman hadn't said as much, but there was a feeling in the dream. Like it was well known that he was dead, and it was my fault. Everything had been my fault.

"This is good. Very good." Zane scribbled fiercely in his book. "Anything else?"

I swallowed hard. "Yes. Snow. Her name was Snow, and she was King Midas' daughter."

Chapter 11

AFTER MY ADMISSION, ZANE had to go check on some things. He swore he'd be back, but it has been three hours and still no sign of him.

My stomach rumbled.

Rubbing it, I frowned.

I probably should get something to eat. I missed breakfast. Plus, at this rate, I was going to need glasses from all the reading.

While there were more than enough references to King Midas, there was no mention of me at all. The book I was looking at now mentioned his daughter Marigold or

Zoe by some accounts, which King Midas apparently turned into gold, but none of a girl named Snow.

Had everything I dreamed been just that, a dream? I hardly thought it possible. There was too much detail. Too many things that lined up just right for them to be just figments of my imagination.

This Snow woman had to go by another name.

I flipped the page too hard, ripping the edge of it.

"Oh, no!" I gasped, my eyes brimming with tears. "That's just wonderful. Zane leaves me alone for just a little bit, and I go and ruin his book. Could today get any worse?"

Pushing my fists into my eyes, I groaned and stretched my back.

"Someone looks like they could use a break."

My hands dropped instantly as I twisted around in my seat and saw Adam walk across the library.

Eyes narrowing, I took in his mused hair and rumbled clothing. I turned back to my book and flipped the next page, but not too hard. "Have a good meeting with Rebecca?" I couldn't help the sharpness in my voice.

Adam sat down in Zane's vacant seat next to me. "If you could call it that." He dragged a hand over his face a bit tiredly. "She tends to ramble on and on about things of no consequence before getting to the point."

My eyes lifted briefly and locked onto the red lip print on his neck. Jaw tightening, I glared down at the book. "And was that point on your neck?"

Out of the corner of my eye, Adam frowned and reached up to his neck, rubbing at the mark. "Oh, yeah, I forgot about that." He made a disgusted face. "Rebecca can get a little over-enthusiastic with her dealings."

I snorted.

"What?"

I shrugged a shoulder. "Nothing. It's just clear that she wants more than to just meet with you." I flipped the page and winced as I heard a slight tear. "She's very forthcoming with her affections every time she sees you."

Not responding to me, I could still feel his eyes on my face. I ducked my head, trying to hide behind my hair.

"Eva."

I ignored him, turning the page without reading it.

"Eva, look at me." His fingers brushed back my hair and tipped my chin up.

I kept my eyes down and then blinked as I lifted my gaze.

Adam's mouth turned up into a small smile, his eyes alight with humor. "Are you jealous? Of Rebecca?"

My lower lip pushed out, and I jerked my head out of his grasp. "No."

The chair scratched against the floor as Adam moved closer to me. His arm went across the back of my chair I shifted forward, so he wasn't touching me. "Eva," he murmured, his other hand brushing my hair behind my ear. "Rebecca means nothing to me. She's in the past-"

My head snapped to him. "Then why do you let her maul you like a court harlot?"

Sighing, Adam looked off to the side. "Remember how I said I had to keep up appearances until I was made Arch Mage?"

I nodded reluctantly. I had a feeling I knew where this was going.

"Well, unfortunately, Rebecca is one of those. I must let her believe I'm still interested if even just a little so she doesn't suspect I might have had a change of heart." He cupped the side of my face with his hand, peering deeply into my eyes.

I licked my lower lip, and his eyes flicked down at the movement. "Have you had a change of heart?"

Adam leaned closer. "Perhaps, if we're careful..." His thumb stroked across my lower lip, and this time I knew he was going to kiss me.

"Hey, Eva! I made lunch. Do you want...some?" Luke trailed off as Adam dropped his hand and sighed. "Was I interrupting something?"

Adam moved away, putting more space between us. "No. We're done here." He gave me a significant look before standing. "I have more work to do." He touched my head, and then before I knew it, his lips were pressed to my forehead. "Don't work too hard. Take a break before you kill yourself."

Straightening, Adam walked toward Luke, my eyes following him the whole way. "Make sure she gets something to eat and does something besides reading those old dusty tomes."

Luke gave us a curious look but then smiled at Adam, giving him a salute. "Will do."

When Adam was gone, Luke shoved his hands into his pockets, pushing his robe to the side. "So, find anything out yet?"

I sighed and looked back to the book I had been taking my anger out on. "No. Nothing of importance." I placed the ribbon bookmark into place and stood. "Adam is right, though. I've been stuck in here for too long."

"Where'd Zane go? I thought he was helping you?" Luke waited for me to make my way over to him before starting for the door.

I shrugged. "Zane said he had to look into some stuff, but then he never came back."

Luke scoffed. "That's just like him."

"What?"

"He gets lost in whatever he is doing and forgets about everyone and everything else." Luke placed his hand on my lower back and pressed close to my side.

My head and heart were getting so confused. Luke had clearly stated his intentions toward me before. Now Adam was showing interest. And if I were to take what transpired between Zane and myself, as well as the demon's words, then he was also a contender.

I only needed Gage and Blake to have a complete set.

Smiling to myself at the thought, I didn't realize Luke was staring at me until we stopped in the hallway. "Is something wrong?"

Luke's lips twitched. "No. Not at all." His gaze shifted from one side of the hallway to the other before he grabbed my hand. "Come here."

Curious at where we were going, I allowed him to lead me into a nearby room.

I hadn't been in this room before. Lined with shelves and filled with boxes, it seemed more of a storage room than anything else. Wondering what we were doing in there, I didn't know the door shut behind us until Luke had me pressed up against a shelf.

"What are you doing?" I murmured, placing my hands on his arms as he wrapped them around my waist.

Luke lifted one hand, his fingers dragging through the lengths of my hair. "I've been thinking about doing this again ever since the first time. Then everything happened, and I didn't think you..."

Realizing what he wanted to do, I flushed and ducked my head. "I do enjoy your company, Luke. And before...when you kissed me...I'd been surprised, but it wasn't unpleasant."

Chuckling, Luke leaned his forehead against mine. "If all you took from my kiss was that it wasn't unpleasant, then I didn't do a good enough job of it."

I lifted my head, my eyes widening as my pulse raced. "No, I didn't mean that at all. I just meant -"

"Shhh." Luke took my chin in his hand. "I know what you meant. Just let me kiss you."

My lips parted as I breathed, "Okay."

His mouth covered mine. My hands shifted from his arms to the front of his shirt as I pressed against him. The hard plains of Luke's muscle beneath his clothing drew a small sound of pleasure from my throat.

That sound must have encouraged Luke because he turned his head slightly and swiped his tongue at my lips. Hesitant at first, I slowly opened my mouth to him. Luke's hand dropped to my hip and the other to the back of my head, pressing us even closer.

Kissing Luke was like finally being able to breathe. All the stress and worry I'd had about the others, about the other Eva, even about Master Tuck, fluttered away like the bird in my tower. We were suspended in that moment, and I couldn't imagine it getting any better than this.

Breaking the kiss, Luke's golden eyes were dark with lust as he peered down at me. "I should have taken you somewhere nicer than the storage room for this, but I couldn't wait."

I smiled, feeling a little lightheaded. "I don't mind."

Luke leaned down and kissed me quickly and passionately once more but broke it soon after, leaving me breathless and wanting. "Come on, we should go eat lunch. Blake's waiting for us."

The reminder that others actually existed caused my cheeks to burn with embarrassment. "Oh, yes. That's probably a good idea."

My body burned with need, and while I was fairly sure I'd already given myself to King Midas, I wasn't quite ready to take that step with Luke. Especially not while my heart was so conflicted about Adam and Zane.

Chapter 12

BLAKE SAT AT THE kitchen island, a plate already in front of him.

"What's that?" I pointed at the triangle-shaped food on his plate. There was a bigger circular version of it on a nearby wooden platter where he'd taken a piece off.

"A food that will always make it through the test of time. Pizza." Luke slid into the seat next to Blake and grabbed a piece. He held it out to me and winked. "Go ahead. Try it."

Peering at the yellow and white melted top and variety of color scattered around, I leaned forward acutely aware of the two sets of eyes on me.

The aroma coming from the bread-like item filled my nostrils and made my mouth water. Opening my mouth slightly, I sank my teeth into the warm gooey food. An explosion of flavors raced across my tongue, and I closed my eyes, moaning in pleasure.

Clearing his throat, Luke said, "Good, right?"

I opened my eyes and swallowed, nodding. "It's delicious. So many different flavors. How did you make it?"

Blake snorted. "He didn't."

My eyes shifted to Blake. "Then did you?"

Luke chuckled and placed the delicious food on a plate and sat it in front of the empty seat beside him. "It was delivered while you were in the library."

I frowned. "How is it still so warm to have been brought from somewhere else?"

With three pieces of pizza on his plate, Luke answered with half of one of them in his mouth. "A stasis spell."

My brows rose. "Like the one that was on me?"

Blake shook his head. "No. The one on you was a more complex combination of a spell and enchanted items - the chains you were wearing at the time." He bit into his pizza, mulling it over. "Zane and I haven't extensively gone over the chains just yet because we haven't been able to get back in the tower."

"Why not?" I sat down on my stool and took another glorious bite of my food. I barely contained my moan of delight.

This time Luke answered. "We don't know. The council closed it off after your hearing with them. We've already submitted a request to access it once more."

"Isn't that a bit..." I trailed off, not wanting to speak badly of the council.

"Suspicious," Blake grunted. "That's the word you're looking for."

Standing, I walked over to the refrigerator. As I opened it, I asked, "What would they be looking for?" I grabbed a bottle of juice and turned back to them. "I mean, what do they expect to learn? There's nothing in there but my chains. Believe me, I know." I laughed bitterly and twisted the cap off.

Luke shrugged. "We don't know if it's them specifically trying to find something. It could be Master Tuck is up to something untoward." He wiped his mouth with a napkin and patted his stomach.

I was in awe of Luke's ability to pack away food. Luke certainly didn't look like he ate the way he did. Neither did Blake, who ate just as much but at a slower pace.

I mused over what they said as I finished off my pizza. What could they want with my tower? My stomach twisted into knots just thinking about it. Having Adam looking into the tower was one thing, the council or even Master Tuck snooping around it was so much worse.

"So," Luke glanced at his brother and me, "want to watch a movie?"

Blake grunted his consent.

"Alright," I hopped off my stool and followed Luke into the living room.

Luke sat on one side of the couch in front of the television and patted the seat next to him. Suddenly shy, I meandered over and sank onto the couch cushion. Luke threw his arm around my shoulder as soon as I sat down, pulling me in close.

I snuggled into his side.

Blake came out of the kitchen shortly later, a bowl of popcorn in his hands. He plopped down on the other side of me. Unlike the times before, Blake didn't force himself to the furthest edge of the couch. Blake sat a comfortable distance away, his thigh brushing mine.

He must have felt my eyes on him because he turned to me. "Popcorn?"

My lip curled up as I groaned. "No, thank you. I'm full."

"I'll take some." Luke grabbed a handful and shoved it into his mouth.

I giggled and shook my head. "You two must have hollow legs."

"We're growing boys," Luke pouted his mouth full of popcorn. "Besides," he smirked down at me. "I worked up an appetite."

I sank further into the couch, my face burning.

Blake gave me a sidelong look but didn't comment.

Thankfully, Luke turned the television on and played a movie about an ogre who saved a princess from a tower. It was funny and romantic, but I only saw about thirty minutes of it before my eyes grew heavy and I fell asleep.

My hands smoothed over my white off the shoulder gown. Cows moaned, and chickens clucked, making me scrunch my nose up in disgust.

Ferdinand was late. I hated waiting.

It was almost ten o'clock. Trying to sneak out of my bedchamber at this time was practically impossible. My mouth twisted in a grimace. Midas always wanted to copulate after too much wine.

Tonight though, I had made sure to add a little extra to one of his nightly glasses of wine.

Midas was out in minutes, making it easy to slip out of our bedroom to meet the prince.

"My love!" Ferdinand called out to me as he hurried quietly into the barn. "Have you been waiting long?"

I forced my face into a pleasant expression and not that of annoyance for having to wait. "No. I just arrived."

"My apologies, I was detained." He wrapped his arms around my waist and drew me close. The dark hair on Ferdinand's head stuck out in odd angles, much different than his usual immaculate appearance.

I frowned. "What kept you?"

Something in my heart broke as an image passed behind Ferdinand's eyes, a black-haired beauty with lips as red as roses before he plastered on a smoldering smile and leaned down to kiss me. "Never you mind. Let's not waste our precious time together on such unimportant matters."

Letting him kiss me, my hands latched onto the sides of his face and pulled him closer as I pushed my powers into him.

I pulled away with a loud smack. Swiping my mouth on the back of my hand, I gave Ferdinand an icy glare. "Now, no more games. Answer me."

Ferdinand's expression went blank. His eyes glazed over. "Whatever you wish, my queen."

"Where were you?"

"I came from the palace," he answered in a monotone voice.

Rage billowed inside of me. "What were you doing at the palace when you just arrived in town tonight?"

"I arrived three days ago, my queen." The more Ferdinand answered my questions, the more I wanted him to shut up. "I spent the last three days making love to the fair Snow. I mean to make her my bride."

My eyes burned with tears while my chest felt like it was being ripped in two.

Never. I had never fallen in love before. I had never allowed myself to. Love was for the weak. And all my energy was needed for my revenge on the mages. I couldn't be distracted by silly things like love.

Not until Prince Ferdinand came to visit last season.

He stood before the court in his formal wear, all reds, blacks, and golds. Bowing before the court at our winter ball, his eyes had lingered on me. Those beautiful deep blue eyes had pierced straight into my hardened heart. We danced that night, many times. Each time I felt my skin come alive with his touch and my heart pounded in my chest like it never had before.

Now we met every fortnight like this, outside of the palace, and away from prying eyes. Ferdinand knew every inch of my body as I knew his...and now apparently did Snow.

Fire burned in my palms as I imaged the lovely face of my stepdaughter. She had been a hindrance to me for the last time.

Turning my attention back to my prince, a cruel smile slid up my lips. "Listen closely, my prince. You will go back to Princess Snow and ask for her hand."

"Yes, my queen."

I imagined the joy on the princess's face as I spoke, of everything she was stealing from me when she already had so much. "Then, after you have said your vows when the whole court is busy celebrating your union, make your excuses so you can wait for me in your chambers." My chin lifted as I finished, "I have a gift I wish to give you both to celebrate your happy day."

Ferdinand smiled calmly, "Thank you, my queen."

"Now go. I do not wish to see or speak to you until that time." I waved a hand, breaking the spell.

Ferdinand frowned, his eyes clearing. "I'm sorry. I have to go." Without waiting for my response, he turned on his heel and left the barn.

When I was alone, I let loose the fire I'd been holding back, and my cackling was the only sound left of the barn after I was finished.

"Eva, Eva," a hand shook my shoulder as I jerked awake.

Blinking my eyes up at Blake, I sat up in confusion. Luke was nowhere to be found.

"My brother had to help a patient," Blake answered my unasked question.

I rubbed my eyes and stretched. "Was I out for long?"

Blake shook his head. "No, but you were laughing in your sleep."

My arms paused overhead. "I was?"

"Yes," he murmured distractedly. His single golden eye lingered over my form, and I dropped my arms with a blush. Standing abruptly, Blake turned his back on me. "I have to get back to work. Zane's back. You should go find him."

I wanted to call out to him but didn't know what to say. He was gone before I could make a decision.

Sighing, I sank back onto the couch. Now what?

"You brazen little hussy."

Chapter 13

SPINNING AROUND, I PUSHED off the couch and to my feet. "Z...Zane? I thought you were waiting in the library?"

Zane sat at the dining table behind the couch, one leg crossed over the other. His hair was unbound and hanging over the shoulders of his unbuttoned shirt, his hand up by his face. We had dimmed the lights for the movie, making it hard to see Zane's face in the shadows.

"A change of scenery," was his response, a red dot illuminating his face in the dark.

"You're not wearing your glasses," I murmured, my pulse picking up speed.

Smoke wafted into the air, the scent making my nose twitch at the unpleasant smell.

Something was wrong. My hair stood on end as I inched away from him, and the room felt like someone had turned up the heat.

"Why do you back away?" A hiss filled the air as the red dot appeared once more followed by the sickly-sweet smell of smoke. "You were so willing to give your affections to the other two, does this one not appeal to you?"

My lips pressed into a thin line as my eyes narrowed. This wasn't Zane.

"What do you want?"

The demon threw his head back and laughed, a cackling sound that was so similar to my dream that it made a shiver go down my spine. "It's not about what I want. It's about the mage."

He dropped his leg, and I flinched.

"I don't think Zane would want you speaking for him," I countered, wishing for the first time that the other Eva would take over now. Why was she only ever here when I didn't want her?

I tried to make my way to the door, moving slowly so as not to alert him to my escape route.

Chuckling darkly, the demon pushed his chair back and stood, the sound of it scraped against the ground. I winced at the grating sound. Zane's possessed body stepped into the dim light allowing me to see the red of his eyes, usually a lovely shade of brown and green. "Our timid mage wouldn't think to speak for himself. He certainly would never just take what he wanted," the demon bit out with a snarl. "It is positively disgusting watching him pine after such a slip of a girl." He waved his hand at me, a rolled white paper in between two fingers. The sickly-sweet smell was coming from the burning end, and I wrinkled my nose.

"You shouldn't be doing that in here." I pointed at it as I moved closer to the door. I was almost there. "You're going to stink the whole house up."

Lifting the rolled paper to his mouth, the demon inhaled, his eyes locked on mine as he did it. He blew out the smoke in my direction with a smirk. "What are you going to do about it?"

I waved a hand in front of me, resisting the urge to cough. The longer I stayed around the scent, the more lightheaded I felt. "I suppose I can't do anything about it. I don't even know what it is." I nodded toward the paper while I pressed my back to the door. "I do know Adam will not be happy if there are charred marks on the floor if you drop it."

Blindly, I searched for the button to open the door. I almost had it when a whoosh of air followed by a slap of a hand on the wall behind me stopped me.

My back tensed as the demon peered down at me through Zane's eyes. Typically, being this close to Zane would have made my stomach feel funny, like spiders crawling around. Still, the deceptively charming expression on his face made me want to punch him.

"This," the demon held up the rolled paper, "is a nifty thing the humans invented a long time ago. Technically, it's not the exact same thing. You can't find tobacco anywhere now. The damnable mages burned it all to the ground with many of the other enjoyable vices the humans so loved." He sighed and wafted the smoke under my nose, making it itch.

I resisted the urge to scratch it, my entire focus on the demon so close to me. "I wouldn't know. I've never seen anything like that before."

The demon's lower lip poked out in a pout. It was quite an unusual expression on Zane's face. "Of course not. It's fifty years or so before your time." He sighed and stared longingly at it. "Still, the mages do have a way of making up for the things they destroy. This lovely herb is called Damiana."

All the smoke was making me feel a bit funny. My head felt fuzzy, and my body was warm. A low burning had begun between my thighs. I pressed them together to try and quell the feeling.

"An interesting little fact about Damiana. While used mostly for healing," the demon caged me in, his hips pressing against mine, "it has aphrodisiac purposes as well. Not that our mage would ever use such a drug for those reasons." He winked creepily. "It doesn't stop me from partaking in it from time to time, though." A small sound crept from my throat as he ground his hips into mine.

If I hadn't been fighting the effects of the smoke, I would have been embarrassed to feel Zane's hardened length pushed against my stomach.

Licking my lips, I put my hands up between us. "I got rid of you once, I can do it again." If only I knew the damn spell word, I'd used before. I hoped the demon wouldn't call my bluff.

Giving me a full toothed smile, he cupped my face with one hand. "Oh, little girl. I smell the lie on you, but I'm not here to play with you today. No, no. Sometimes I just want to cause a little chaos." He winked once more before the red of his eyes changed to the pretty brown-green of Zane's.

I expected Zane to pass out on me like he always did. Except he didn't. Those intelligent eyes blinked several times before focusing on me.

Perhaps it was because the demon left on its own rather than being forced out, or the demon wanted Zane to stay awake. Still, the moment Zane realized the position we were in, he jerked away, stumbling over his feet.

"Oh, Eva. I'm...I'm so sorry. He didn't hurt you, did he?" Zane's eyes were wide and full of fear. His arm tensed like he wanted to come to me, but he kept his distance.

Finally, safe from the demon, my body rejected the smoke, causing me to cough and sneeze repeatedly.

Zane stared at me for a moment until I pointed at the drug still in his hand. He muttered a curse and then a few words I didn't understand before the white paper and herb burned up instantly.

"Better?"

I nodded. "Yeah. Thanks." I wiped my nose on the back of my hand and sighed. "And no. He didn't hurt me."

Sagging on the ground, Zane's eyes stayed down to the floor. "I thought...our position...he tried to..."

My head shook and rushed to kneel beside him. "No, he didn't. I think..." I blinked down at the ground, my face heating. "He was trying to..." I pointed a finger between the two of us and then jerked my head toward his pants.

Zane cleared his throat and straightened slightly. "I apologize. I would never put you in such a position-"

"Do you want to kiss me?" I blurted out of nowhere.

Giving me a startled frown, Zane cocked his head to one side, his blood-red hair falling over his face. "Do I want to kiss you? Why would you...I mean...did he say something? Because whatever it was just-"

I leaned forward and pressed my lips to Zane's promptly cutting off his rambling.

A moment later, I pulled back and sat on my heels, watching and waiting to see how he would react.

His eyes fluttered open, mouth ajar as he processed what had just happened. Then his face turned as red as his hair as he cleared his throat and re-buttoned the buttons on his shirt. "Why...I..."

I smiled brightly at him. He was just so flustered and adorable. It made me want to kiss him again. Instead of torturing him more, I stood and offered him my hand, "How about we go check some more of the books? I had another dream. So, we might be able to find something else based on that."

Clearly thankful for the change of subject, Zane slid his hand into mine and stood, putting him close to me. There was a new tension now between us that hadn't been there before, and while I was still confused about who I cared for more, the way Zane was smiling down at me, I couldn't say I regretted it.

Chapter 14

BY THE END OF the week, Blake had made a regular habit of being the first person I saw when I made my way up the servants' stairs. He never came down to my room except to drop items off, and I was never there when he did it.

This time, Blake waited at the top of the stairs, Izzy noticeably missing from his side. Eying me with a - if possible, grumpier than usual expression, Blake pushed off the wall and shoved his hands in his pockets. "Come on, we're going to be late."

Confused, I hurried after him. I wondered if I would be getting breakfast on this little excursion.

We were out the front door and down the walkway before I finally caught up to Blake. It was early enough that the streets weren't busy, so I was able to walk side by side with him.

"Are you going to tell me where we're going, or am I supposed to guess?"

Blake stopped abruptly and turned. His single golden eye looked down at me. "We're going shopping." He continued walking again, and I had to hurry to keep up with him.

"For?"

We turned a corner into a more crowded area. With an annoyed grunt, I slowed my stride so that I trailed behind Blake like all the other humans did for their mages. I dipped my head but eyed the area around us as we passed.

Humans walked together or slightly behind their mages, some holding bags full of items. In contrast, others laced their fingers together in front of them as if they were children in a store. A few of them shot looks my way as Blake and I passed by, curious about the new human in the area.

I hadn't been out of the house or around the city since the visit from the council, and that had only been a car ride. I hadn't gone around on foot since Luke took me to get my hair cut.

My fingers subconsciously trailed through the ends of my hair.

Blake, unlike his brother, was a quiet companion. He didn't offer up information about the area, or point out funny things for me to laugh about. We sluiced through the crowds at a moderate pace, his eyes never going back to me to make sure I was keeping up.

A few mages bumped me on their way by. None of them apologized, but every single one of them gave me a dirty look as if it was my fault for being in their way.

By the time we made it to the shop Blake wanted, a heaviness had pressed on my chest, and the underlying burn of the other Eva's magic boiled in the pit of my stomach.

Stepping up close to Blake, I lowered my voice and whispered hotly, "This is not a good idea."

Blake angled a look at me from the corner of his eye, a frown on his lips. "Why?"

I shook my head venomously, my gaze darting around. "There's too many of them. I don't know if I can control her."

Pursing his lips, Blake took me by the elbow and directed me into the store. "It'll be fine. Come on."

For the first time, I noticed what kind of store we were at.

A dress shop.

Lines and lines of dresses filled the store. All shapes and colors, some even flickered from one color to the next on their stands. Mages strolled down the dresses, their humans trailing after them some with their arms piled with garments.

I swallowed thickly. My awe of the gowns overtaken by my panic. This couldn't be good. The last shop I was in, the shopkeeper yelled at me. With how close the other Eva already was to the surface, it wouldn't take much to cause a scene, and then I would be outed and back in my tower in no time.

Blake stepped up to one of the racks of dresses and flipped through them quickly. He'd pause every once in a while, to look one over before flicking it aside. Not once did he ask my opinion or explain why we were there.

A woman with her hair, the color of coral, curled in a strange kind of spiral on her head, approached us. Her eyes never went to me, her focus entirely on Blake. "Can I help you find something?"

"No," Blake clipped, not once acknowledging her.

The woman's smile wilted for a moment before coming back in full force as she cleared her throat. "We have several new items in the back. Perhaps you would like to take a look at them?"

This time Blake didn't even answer, only grunted.

Her eyes darted sideways to me, the first proof she even knew I existed, her cheeks tinging pink.

Instead of dipping my head like I was supposed to, I stared at her straight on, defiant. Annoyance crossed her face, feeding the flame inside of me. The other Eva pushed at my consciousness, and I felt my mouth open to say something I shouldn't, I was sure, but I never got it out.

"This one." Blake shoved a lavender gown into my arms and jerked his arm to the side. "Go put it on."

The shop woman made a startled sound but wisely didn't protest.

I hesitated for a moment, the urge to give the woman a piece of my mind almost too strong to resist.

Blake noticed my conflict and turned to the woman. "Go away."

My lips ticked up at the surprise on her face. I stifled my laughter in the material of the gown, hiding my face from onlookers.

The woman glanced between the two of us for a second before huffing and stalking away. She stopped at a counter where other workers stood and began talking to them in a low but adamant voice. A hand pushed at my back.

I slid my gaze over to Blake.

"Go," he commanded, nodding his head toward a set of doors. "Try it on."

My lips twisting to the side, I walked over to the doors and tried one that had green letters lit up reading 'Open' across the front. There were curious eyes on me until I stepped inside and closed the door.

Apparently, this was not a normal circumstance.

Taking a deep breath, I let it out slowly.

At least in here, I had a reprieve from all the stares and grumbles. The other Eva no longer pushed on my mind, but I could still feel her there. Watching. Waiting. She was content for the moment to see how things unfolded.

Pulling one arm and then the other out of my dress, I gazed at the garment Blake had chosen for me.

Lavender in color, it was long in the back but short in the front. The skirt had several layers of fabric that puffed up on the sides. It reminded me of rose petals. The top half was off the shoulder with a slight slit in the middle. It really was a gorgeous piece of work.

I couldn't figure out why Blake would want me to wear such a gown. I couldn't clean the house in it. I certainly didn't have anywhere to wear such an outfit.

But as I slid the gown over my skin, the feel of it like a lover's caress, I didn't care. I wanted this gown.

It fit me as if it were made for me. The top cupped my breasts until they were pushed up but not obscenely so. The waist of the gown laid snug against my skin without being too constricting. The skirt, which I had worried would show off too much leg, had a fitted skirt beneath the flower poof.

So lost in admiring the feel of the dress, I forgot the whole reason I was in there until a bang on the door jolted me.

"Do you need help?" Blake asked cautiously.

"Uh, no." I smoothed my hands over the fabric once more with a smile. "It fits fine."

There was a pause, and then Blake demanded, "Come out."

My brows drawn together, I opened the door and stepped out into the store.

Though wrapped in layers of cloth, I felt utterly exposed as almost every eye in the store zeroed in on me, including Blake's.

I laced my fingers in front of me and shifted from side to side, trying to play the dutiful human. "Well?"

Blake devoured every inch of me with his gaze, not speaking for a long moment. Then he lifted his hand and snapped his fingers.

A shop worker quickly appeared at his side, a different one than before. "Yes? What can I do for you?" Her gaze skittered over to me, and she pursed her lips tightly, clearly dying to say something about a human wearing their clothing.

Blake didn't spare her a glance. "We'll take this dress. Do you have shoes..." he trailed off, waving a hand at me. "That'll match?"

"Of course, sir." She nodded quickly and disappeared into another section of the store.

When she was gone, I sighed and muttered to Blake, "Everyone is staring."

He snorted. "Let them."

"But I shouldn't be doing this, should I?" I tried once more to make him see how this was a bad idea. Even though I had no idea what we were even doing in the shop to begin with.

Huffing in annoyance, Blake's golden gaze locked with mine. "Adam told me to find you a gown. That is what I'm doing. What they think is irrelevant."

I wished I had his indifference to everyone around us. I hadn't been in this time for long, but I knew I wanted to fit in. Even if I didn't want to play the human servant part. Almost anything was better than going back to my tower. Almost.

The woman returned shortly with the shoes. Reluctantly, she placed them on the floor before me.

Unsure if I was allowed to speak or not, I shot a look at Blake. "They seem a bit big."

"They won't be," Blake answered flippantly.

Shrugging in response, I stepped into the shoes. Instantly, they shrank to fit my feet. I gasped in surprise.

The shop woman sniffed, offended by my reaction. "All of our clothing is enchanted to fit the wearer. We're not some human shop." Realizing what she'd said and who she'd said it to, she covered her mouth with her hand and sent Blake a worried look.

Blake's head jerked in her direction, the black and white hair on his head shifting to reveal the purple of his other eye and the scar that crossed it. The shop woman made a keening sound, her face going white.

"My apologies," she quickly stuttered out and practically ran away from us.

Once we had paid for our purchase, a different worker claimed the dress and shoes would be delivered to the house. Blake stalked out of the shop and I arched a brow at Blake. "Do all people respond like that?"

Blake grunted, his footsteps hurried, even more so than when we left the house.

The silence between us was tense all the way back. I waited until we were safe behind the doors of the house before I grabbed Blake by the arm.

"Would you stop?"

Letting out a long sigh, Blake spun around to me, his face pinched with annoyance. "What?"

I stepped up to him, making sure to keep my eyes on his as I reached out. He flinched but didn't move away from me as I brushed his hair out of his face. The glowing purple eye stared down at me cautiously as if waiting for me to react the way the shop worker did.

Stroking my finger along the edges of his scar, I murmured, "You don't have to hide from me, Blake."

His eyes closed briefly. "But my scar..."

"Is just a scar." I smiled as he opened his eyes once more. "Believe me, even though you can't see them, I have them too. It doesn't make you less."

I didn't need to know my whole past to know that the other Eva had some deep wounds. If only she'd had someone to help her heal, rather than having them fester? Would the prince and king still be alive? I had to believe she never would have ended up in that tower had someone been there for her. Like I was for Blake.

A much larger hand cupped mine as Blake murmured, "Thank you."

Chapter 15

BLAKE HAD TO GO work on some conjuring spell and left me in the kitchen after making me some of the fluffiest, tastiest pieces of bread ever. He called them pancakes, but to me, they were heaven.

Adam walked in while I had my mouth filled to the brim with pancakes. He took one look at me and smirked, "Hungry?"

Smiling around the food, I tried to say, "Starving," but it came out all muffled and incoherent. Chewing quickly, I grabbed the glass of milk sitting before me and downed a few gulps. With a sigh of pleasure, I tried again. "Yes. I am. These are really exceptional." I dug my fork into another bite and moaned.

All things that are holy and good. I'd sell my firstborn for some pancakes.

Chuckling at me, Adam leaned against the edge of the counter. "Did you have a nice trip to the shops?"

I snorted around my food.

Eyebrows raising, Adam hummed. "That's unfortunate. I hoped it would be a nice experience for you. Getting to try on pretty dresses."

"It would have been had it not been for all the staring. Also, Blake picked my dress out. I didn't really get much of a say in it." I pointed my fork at him before stabbing another bite.

Adam sighed. "Yes, well, that is why I asked him to take you. Blake does have an eye for women's fashion. Though he was supposed to give you a choice."

I shook my head. "It's fine. He probably wanted to get out of there as quickly as I did."

"It was that bad?"

I grimaced. "Not really. Just uncomfortable. You know, pretending to be a servant with all the walking behind and keeping my eyes down. Then, of course, the mages weren't very nice to me, and that put the other Eva into a tizzy."

Adam's face went serious. "She didn't emerge, did she?"

I swallowed the mouthful of milk as I jerked my head back and forth. "No. Well, almost, but Blake helped defuse the situation."

"That's good." Adam relaxed.

We were quiet for a few moments. Me eating my pancakes and Adam watching me eat. It was a little unnerving to be certain.

To fill the void, I blurted out, "What's the dress for anyway?"

"Oh? Blake didn't tell you?"

I laughed bitterly. "That seems to be happening a lot today. Just when I was starting to like him too."

Adam's brows rose. "You are?"

My cheeks grew hot. "We're getting off the topic."

Eyes laughing, Adam shifted around, so his arm leaned against the counter. "Of course. We can't have that. And to answer your question, every year, we have a council Gala."

I frowned. "A Gala?"

"Like a ball." Adam sighed and dragged a hand through his silver hair. "It's basically just an excuse to dress up and get drunk while trying to find political advantages with the other members of the council. Obviously, since I am not only the Arch Mage's grandson but also in the running for successor, I have to make an appearance. As well as the rest of the household."

"Alright," I drew out, still not understanding my part in all this. "But why am I going?"

"Because you are my guest and new to this world."

Narrowing my eyes at him, I asked pertly, "Are any of the other mages bringing their humans along?"

Adam's mouth twisted to the side. "Well, no, but if we are going to figure out who you are, having you there to help ask questions will make it easier. Besides, I've already cleared it with my grandfather. So, there's no use trying to find excuses."

I opened my mouth and then clipped it shut with a growl.

Stepping closer to me, Adam brushed my hair behind my ear. "Also, perhaps, I want to see you all dressed up like you were in your time."

"My time?"

Adam's lip ticked up. "You were a queen after all, weren't you?"

The other Eva was a queen. A bitter queen with a grudge. I wasn't so sure I could fill those shoes even with enchanted ones.

"Very well." I finally gave in with a sigh. "I guess you don't leave me a choice."

"That's right." Adam smacked the table with a cheerful grin. "I'm not. Also, I wanted to discuss your position in this household."

"My position?" I arched a brow. "I thought I was to be your servant, cleaning person, whatever." I waved a hand in the air with my fork and then glanced down at my plate and frowned.

They were gone. Damn. I should have savored them more. Perhaps I could persuade Blake to make them for me again?

"Well, yes," Adam's cheeks tinted red, and I couldn't help but notice how appealing he looked that way. "But it was only to appease the council and get that nosy Master Tuck off our backs. Now that Zane has tightened the wards, we don't have to pretend besides outside of this house. Also, I do believe finding out about your past takes precedence over things like cooking and cleaning." Adam rolled his eyes and smiled. "We've been doing okay for ourselves for this long, I think we can manage again."

I laughed. "Well, seeing as I wasn't that good at either of those things, I think you are getting the better bargain."

"Could be." Adam's eyes twinkled with laughter.

Our eyes locked for a long moment that caused the air to thicken with tension. Every time things ended up this way, Adam would take one step forward and then five steps back, hurting me in the process. This time I made sure I was the one to break our connection first.

Clearing my throat, I shifted on my stool as I gathered my dishes. I could at least wash them. It was the polite thing to do after all.

I didn't make it to the sink.

A crash from the other side of the house jolted me, and I dropped the plate, sending it smashing to the ground. I knelt for it, but Adam grabbed my arm.

"Leave it. We'll clean it up later." Without an explanation, he pulled me out of the kitchen and down the hall. Another crash followed by a curse, and a groan led us down a hallway I recognized.

The room I'd been using before was down this way. I longed for that room again. The balcony overlooking the city. The shower. I reminded myself to ask Adam if I could move back into it now that we weren't playing pretend anymore.

"Shit. Gage." Adam grunted and released me to hurry toward an open bedroom door.

My footsteps faltered at the giant mage's name. I still hadn't come face to face with the mage since I played my trick on him. A familiar fear gripped my throat, but I pushed it down.

I couldn't avoid him forever. I had to get it over with. Besides, Adam looked worried. He might need my help.

Pushing the door to the room open, I stepped cautiously inside. The room was tidy. Not too large or small. Unlived in would be my best description except for the messy bed and the broken glass all over the floor.

Adam swiped his hand, a magical force swept over the glass, picking it up and dumping it in the trash. He knelt before Gage, who could barely stay on the edge of the bed. Gage's face, the half you could see not covered by his mask, was covered in blood and festering boils, Gage swatted an angry hand out at Adam.

"I'm fine. Leave off."

Rolling his eyes, not at all put off by the large man, Adam produced a cloth out of thin air. He wiped at Gage's face, cleaning some of the blood off. "You're obviously not fine. Or else you wouldn't have broken your favorite clock."

"It was in the way," Gage muttered and then had a coughing fit so hard he began to fall off the bed.

Adam grabbed him around the middle and moved him further onto the bed until the giant mage was lying down. "See? You need help occasionally."

"Screw you," Gage croaked in between coughs.

I stepped closer to the bed but not close enough for Gage's reach. "What's wrong with him?"

Shifting his gaze from Gage, Adam gave me a small bitter smile. "He's been cursed."

"Cursed?" I gasped, looking over Gage's form once more. "Why would anyone want to curse him?"

Well, actually, with his prickly personality, I could figure quite a few people would want to curse the mage.

Gage coughed and sat up to peer at me through swollen eyes. "Because I was trying to kill them, Princess."

"Actually," Adam smirked, trying to lighten the mood. "Eva's a queen."

Gage glanced from Adam to me and shook his head. "No wonder she's too good to clean the floors."

I flushed at the reference to our last encounter.

Adam filled Gage in on what had been going on while he was gone as he cleaned up as much of his face as he could. I stood by dumbly, unsure of what I could do to help or if Gage would even take it.

"I'm going to need Lucas for this," Adam sighed and then looked to me. "Will you make sure he doesn't try to get up while I go get him?"

"Oh, I can go get him," I rushed to say, not wanting to be alone with the glowering mage.

Adam shook his head. "No, you can't. He's with a client on the other side of the city. It'll be faster if I teleport. Just sit with him.

That's it." Adam stood, and I shifted into his place a bit reluctantly. "And don't touch him, I'm not sure if it's a spreading curse yet or not."

"And yet you touched me." Gage laughed but ended up coughing instead.

Shrugging a shoulder, Adam smiled. "What can I say? I like to live dangerously."

Gage rolled his one good eye. "Which is what will shorten your life one day."

Watching the exchange between the two of them put me more at ease. I didn't know if it was the playful banter in the midst of a crisis or because the focus was taken off me. Either way, I appreciated the reprieve.

"I'll be back in a jiffy," Adam told me, pointing a finger at Gage. "Don't let that bastard out of bed for nothing."

"Alright," I said with a bit more confidence than I had.

Tension fell over the room the moment Adam left. I sat on the edge of Gage's bed as far away from him as I could get my eyes down on my hands.

"So, you're a queen, huh?" Gage interrupted the silence a bit later.

Chewing my lower lip, I lifted my gaze to his. "Yes."

"Queen of what?"

I shrugged. "Don't know."

"Well, that's not very useful, is it?" Gage groaned and shifted as if to get up.

I held my hands out. "Adam said -"

"Yeah, yeah." Gage waved me off. "I know what his highness said. I'm not getting up. I just need to change positions."

I lowered my hands. "Oh."

True to his words, Gage shifted into a more comfortable position and then laid back down with a sigh. "So, what else have I missed? Make a fool out of anyone else?"

Groaning inwardly, I settled into my fate. This was going to be a long day.

Chapter 16

I SHIFTED UNCOMFORTABLY ON the bed. Where the hell was Luke and Adam?

Gage was quiet for the most part, but when he wasn't coughing, his eyes were scouring my skin in a rather unnerving manner. What on Earth was he looking for?

"You don't like me, do you?"

My head jerked up, and my gaze skittered over to Gage's brown eyes. "What do you mean? I like you fine."

Behind the cloth over his mouth, Gage's lips twitched ever so slightly. Had I not been staring right at him, I'd have missed it.

"There's no need to pretend here." Gage groaned and shifted on his side. "I'm not exactly the most likeable person myself."

I opened my mouth to reply, but Gage had another coughing fit. The cloth of the mask grew damp with some dark spatter.

That couldn't be good.

"You should take your mask off."

Gage's eyes narrowed suspiciously. "I never take my mask off."

"You'll breath better until they come if you take it off." Against my better judgment, I reached out and tried to remove it.

Lightning fast, Gage's hand latched onto my wrist, holding it tight enough to warn but not hurt. "My mask keeps me anonymous from my prey so they do not come after my family if someone should see me."

Sighing in annoyance, I tried to pull my arm away, but he held on tight. "I'm not the enemy or your prey. So why does it matter if I see your face?"

"That is yet to be decided," Gage clipped, shoving my arm back at me.

I rolled my eyes. "Stop acting like a child. I simply don't want you to die because you couldn't breathe through the mask." A thought came to me, and I smirked. "You're not hideously disfigured under there, are you? A crooked tooth? Perhaps a bulbous nose?"

Gage's brows shot up before his eyes narrowed. "No. I'm not disfigured," he sneered. "Women find me quite appealing."

"Oh?" I arched a brow. "You actually attract women with your winning personality? That's hard to believe."

"And you?" Gage countered, waving a hand at me. "You might look like an angel, but you're a little devil. Tricking men into helping you and then leaving them to their fates."

"Finally!" I threw my hands up in the air. "I was wondering when you were going to bring that up. Come on, what's it going to be? Tell me. Cause the anticipation has been killing me."

Cocking his head to the side, Gage stared at me curiously. "You've been waiting this whole time for me to retaliate?"

I shifted away from him, crossing my arms over my chest. "No. Not the whole time."

Gage's laugh startled me back around.

His head thrown back, and his eyes closed tightly, the act lit up his whole face, even behind the mask. My lips twitched and I began giggling as well. That was until Gage started coughing once more.

I grimaced and reached a hand out to touch his arm. "I'm sorry. Does it hurt very much?"

Gage shrugged. "I've had worse."

Frowning at his answer, I wondered how much worse things could have gotten for him. Just the very thought of causing pain to anyone made my stomach twist into knots.

To my utter horror, I realized I had caused someone pain. I'd killed someone. Or Queen Eva had. Bile rose in the back of my throat at the very thought. I tried not to think about how she killed the prince, but it was hard to keep the thoughts out of my head.

"What's wrong?"

I opened my eyes at Gage's voice, pushing back the pain. "Nothing. Just thinking."

Gage had a suspicious look on his face again, but he didn't probe further.

Thankfully, Adam and Luke arrived, saving me from Gage's searching eyes.

"Sorry it took so long." Adam slid into position next to Gage with Luke on the other side. "Luke couldn't just leave his client right away."

Luke winced. "Demorphification spells are tricky. Once you start, you can't really stop, or someone ends up with an arm on their head and an ass for a face."

Gage chuckled, which turned into a cough. "Don't make me laugh."

I stood and backed away from the bed, waiting at the doorway while they asked Gage questions. What did the spell look like when casted? How did he feel? Were there any other skin abnormalities? On and on it went as Luke poked and prodded Gage's body.

At one point, Luke reached for Gage's face mask but stopped, his eyes darting to me. "Uh, Eva. Please don't take offense, but could you wait outside for a minute?"

"Oh." I straightened from the wall and nodded. "Sure. Of course."

I didn't get a step out the door before Gage said, "Wait. Stop."

Pausing, I turned back, our eyes locking.

"You can stay."

Chewing on my bottom lip, I asked, "Are you sure?"

Gage nodded. "I'm sure."

Adam and Luke exchanged a look before Luke returned to the task at hand. I kept my eyes down on the ground, trying not to make it seem as important as it felt to see under Gage's mask. I could feel his gaze on me the whole time, waiting for me to react to his uncovered face.

Eventually, I couldn't take it anymore. My heart pounded as my gaze slid up the bed and over Gage's chest. A defined jawline with a hint of stubble came into view. A dimple in his chin played on my pulse, making me gasp.

Bite-able full lips quirked up at my reaction, and I forced myself to school my features as my eyes lifted once more.

A slightly crooked nose was the only part of Gage's face that could be defined as a blemish, and even that only added to his impressive features. Even covered in boils which Luke was gently removing with his magic, Gage was no doubt the most attractive of all of the mages in the household.

"Well?"

My attention jerked to his eyes. "Well, what?"

"Am I hideously disfigured?"

Annoyance took the place of the awe I'd felt for Gage's looks. I cocked my hip to the side and crossed my arms over my chest. "I can see now why you need to hide your face."

"Why's that?" Gage winced as Luke finished up on his face making him even more beautiful with each moment.

I waved a hand in his direction and scowled. "It'd be hard to stay hidden with looks like that. You'd never be able to kill anyone."

Gage snorted. "Have you ever given a compliment before in your life?"

"Of course. But just to people who deserve it."

"And I don't? I've been cursed, woman." Gage gasped and shifted on the bed. Luke had finished his face and had moved onto his chest.

"And yet you are still being a jerk."

Adam watched the exchange between us with a playful smile on his lips. Luke was too engrossed in his task to pay us much mind, but I had no doubt he'd be relayed what happened by Adam later.

"Ugh, no wonder they put you in that tower." Gage sat up, breathing heavily as Luke cleared out his lungs. "I would too if only to stop your incessant talking. You're such a human. No mage would act this way, you should just -"

"Gage." The warning in Adam's voice cut Gage off, but it was too late. He'd already awakened the other Eva.

"Who did you kill this time? A mother? A child?" The words spit from my lips with a venomous hiss. "Do you even ask what they've done before you play the council's puppet?"

My feet moved forward on their own accord. I was helpless to the other Eva. I couldn't stop her. She wanted pain. She wanted Gage to eat his words as well as his tongue.

I made it as far as the edge of his bed before Adam jumped up. The other Eva didn't like him either and smiled slyly. Power built up in my hand as she cackled, "What luck I have! Three mages, one -"

"Sleep." Adam pressed two fingers to my forehead, and everything went dark.

When I awoke, I was back in my room in the servants' quarters. Groaning, I rolled over and found myself tangled in my sheets. Fighting to get my arms and legs out, I twisted and turned until I ended up on the floor.

"Ouch." I rubbed my butt where I'd landed and ripped the sheets from my form with a huff.

The door of my room banged open, and Adam rushed in. Seeing me on the ground, he rushed to my side. "Are you alright?"

"Yes," I said irritably, shoving the sheets away. It took me a moment to realize why I was in my room. "Is Gage alright?"

Adam nodded. "Yeah. Gage will be fine. Grumpy and stuck on bed rest but fine." His brown eyes searched my face. "Are you, you?"

I frowned and felt for the other Eva. "Yes. She's gone, for now." I huffed a laugh and drew my legs up, laying my forehead on my knees. "I don't know how much more of this I can take, Adam. I'm a danger to all of you. I could have seriously hurt you."

"No, you couldn't. Not really." Adam placed a hand on my head.

My head jerked up, tears brimming my eyes. "Yes. I could have. I could have killed you all, right then and there. She wanted to. I could feel it." I curled my hand into a fist in front of my chest. "I can still feel her anger right here, and it hurts. It hurts so much."

Adam stroked my hair and cupped my cheek. "I know, and we'll figure out how to get rid of her, I promise. But what real harm can she do? A fork in the hand is one thing, but she was weaponless in a room with three powerful mages. What was she going to do?" Adam chuckled. "Beat us to death with these little hands?"

He picked up my hands and pressed a kiss to each one.

I swallowed hard, wanting so badly to tell him the rest but unable to get it out. The other Eva must have done something to keep me from saying it. I could barely even think about the fact that I had magic, let alone try and form the words.

If I knew how to show Adam, I would have right then and there. As it was, there was nothing I could do but nod my head and hope that Adam was right, and I could keep the other Eva from killing the very men who had come to mean so much to me.

Chapter 17

BLAKE STOOD BEHIND ME in the full-length mirror, his calculating gaze moving over me. "We have to do something with your hair."

I shifted self-consciously, pushing a strand of white-blonde hair behind my ear. "You don't think it looks too...ostentatious?" I stared at the dress in the mirror.

The dress shop had dropped it off this morning, and the others insisted that I put it on even though the Gala wasn't for another four hours.

"Women take time to get ready," was what Adam said.

A few days ago, when I had tried the dress on initially, it hadn't looked silly at all. Now, though, it seemed too poufy—too attention-grabbing.

"You look fine." Blake gathered my hair up off the base of my neck. "Believe me, there will be others wearing more obnoxious outfits than yours."

I sighed. "I'm still not so sure about this. Everyone is going to stare."

"So what?"

I locked eyes with Blake in the mirror. "What if someone says something to piss the other Eva off?"

Blake's lips ticked at the edges. "I hope she does get pissed off."

My mouth twisted to the side as I gave him a stern look. "Seriously? That's not helpful. I'm trying not to get locked away again."

"I agree with Blake." I glanced over my shoulder in the mirror to see Luke leaning on the door frame. "Those nitwits need to be brought down a peg or two. What better way than by a human?"

I snorted. "And who'll save me when they lock me away and throw away the key?"

"We will, of course." Luke pushed off the door and walked up behind me. "You need to pin that with the thicker pins, not the thin metal ones. Her hair is too thick for those."

Blake shot his brother a look of contempt over his shoulder. "I know what I'm doing. I did Sabriel's hair all the time."

"And it ended up destroyed within an hour," Luke pointed out with a knowing smirk.

"That's because she would pull it out, not because of me."

My head went back and forth between the two of them. "Who's Sabriel?"

"Our sister," they said at the same time.

I tilted my head to the side. "I didn't know you had a sister."

Luke picked up a piece of my hair and held it up for Blake. "We actually have four."

My eyes bugged out of my head. "Four sisters?"

"Yep," Luke popped the word and grinned. "Growing up was interesting, for sure."

"And we're the youngest," Blake grumbled as he twisted my hair one way and then pinned it. "We were basically living dolls to them."

I tried to imagine that. The two of them as little boys being dressed up like little girls. It made me extremely happy.

"Don't smile like that," Luke poked me in the face. "It's not going to happen."

"What?" I blinked innocently up at him. "I wasn't thinking about anything."

Blake grunted. "Sure you weren't."

"You'd think being the only boys were bad enough," Luke explained with a huff. "But being twins and the youngest meant we were subjected to all kinds of things."

"Aw, you two were probably just the most adorable." I leaned forward to pinch his cheek, but Blake pulled my hair, making me scowl. "Ow!"

"Sorry," he grumbled but smirked in the mirror.

"Hey, don't get me wrong," Luke squatted on the floor in front of me, checking out my shoes. "There were benefits to having so many sisters."

"Like what?" I cocked my head to the side curiously.

Luke's fingers curled around my ankle and slid up my calf, causing a delightful shiver to run through me. "Like how to talk to women," Luke blinked up at me beneath his lashes, a heat in his eyes that made my mouth water.

"How to touch a woman." Blake's fingers trailed along the side of my neck.

I gasped and then swallowed, my heartbeat racing. "I bet that's useful."

Fingers tickled the back of my knee, and my leg jerked involuntarily. "Blake and I had to learn to play with one another if we wanted to do anything boys usually did. We play very well together..."

"Oh." My breath caught in my throat at his implication, and my eyes darted to the mirror, where they locked with Blake's one golden eye. There was something in his expression that I hadn't seen on him before. Blake had shown me indifference, annoyance, and even at times, kindness. Still, he had never shown me anything close to the intense desire he was showing me now.

The hand in my hair slid to the back of my neck, cupping the base, and angling it back. I closed my eyes briefly, a burning growing between my thighs.

"Are you about ready, Eva? I thought we would get there kind of early so we could -" Adam stopped in the room, taking in the situation. "Apparently, I'm interrupting something. I'll just come back."

Luke jumped up from his spot on the ground. "No, you're not. I need to go check on Gage anyway before we leave." He gave me one last hot look before stalking across the room.

Blake went back to pinning my hair as if nothing had happened.

Taking a deep breath to shake off the feelings inside, I angled my head toward Adam. "What were you saying?"

Adam closed the distance between us so he could lean over and looked in the mirror as well. "Forget it, I just want to take you in as you are right now."

I flushed as Adam devoured every inch of me with his eyes. "Stop. I look ridiculous."

"I told her she didn't." Blake tugged on a strand of my hair playfully before pinning the last piece up. "I'm going to check in with Gage as well."

I tilted my head to the side as Blake's fingers lingered along the back of my neck. "Thank you."

"Not a problem." Blake smiled slightly and then slipped from the room.

It was strange. I missed his hands on me already.

"Are you nervous?"

"What?" I spun around, my skirt spinning with me.

Adam had changed clothing already. His usual forest green jacket had been exchanged for a rather formal looking jacket with large shoulder pads and golden frill falling off the sides. An almost black green tie peeked out of the neck of the coat—the buttons of the jacket done up to just below the tie's knot.

I eyed the matching gloves on his hands and smiled. "I guess I'm not the only being dressed up like a doll."

Adam adjusted his gloves and leered at me. "Perhaps later we can discard our costumes together."

I pulled my lower lip into my mouth and ducked my head. "I thought you were supposed to be playing the dutiful member of the council?"

Leaning in close, his mouth brushing my ear, he whispered, "Maybe I think you're worth the risk."

When I lifted my head, our faces were a hair's breadth apart. I licked my lips and let my eyes flutter closed—three different kisses from three different men over the span of a few days. I wondered if the other Eva ever imagined such a thing happening.

The thought of the other Eva and her need to inflict pain on the mages caused me to pause.

Just as Adam's lips caressed mine, I pulled back my eyes snapping open.

"What is it?"

I shook my head and smiled sadly. "We can't. Tonight's important, right?"

Adam arched a brow. "Yes?"

I reached up and straightened out the tie at his neck. "Then you probably shouldn't come there smelling like a human."

"Oh," Adam clipped. "Right." He closed his eyes and bobbed his head, dragging a hand through his silver locks. "You're right. You're so right. I'm sorry."

Smoothing my hands over his jacket, I kept my eyes down and distracted. "It's fine. Don't we need to leave soon?"

Huffing, Adam twisted his hand until the top of his wrist showed. A thin band wrapped around the smallest part and, at the movement, shined a light on Adam's skin, reading the time. "Yes, unfortunately."

He offered me his arm and gave me a meaningful look. "Are you ready for this?"

Was I ready to be on display in a room full of people who hated me and my kind? No. Not now and not ever.

Was I going to go anyway? Yes. Adam and the others were trying to change the way the council viewed the humans, and I'd be damned if I didn't do my part to make it happen.

Mouth dry, I cleared my throat and said, "As long as the other Eva keeps in her corner, yes."

Adam chuckled. "You and me both, but let's be honest, we're going into enemy territory for her. The likelihood that's going to happen is microscopic."

I sighed. "That's true." Forcing my shoulders back, I looped my arm through Adam's offered one. "Let's go before I change my mind."

Adam led me out of the room and up to the front area where all but Gage was waiting.

The twins didn't seem to have a problem dressing similarly because their robes were swapped out for jackets similar to Adam's but in black and white with gold embellishments. When I appeared, they both glanced my way, desire clear in both of their eyes.

Zane had his hair down loose around his shoulders, his glasses sitting on his nose as he peered over at me. Appreciation glimmered in his gaze, and I blushed. The only difference in his clothing was the jacket he had placed over his button-up shirt and tie the same color of his hair around his neck.

"Are we ready to go?" Zane asked, his question for Adam, but his eyes were all for me.

I felt utterly ridiculous in my outfit, and yet the way these men looked at me made it all worthwhile.

"Like I say every year," Adam winked at me. "Let's get this over with."

Chapter 18

THE CAR RIDE HAD to be the longest one in existence. If Blake hadn't assured me the dress was enchanted to soak up any moisture, I would have been worried about sweating through the fabric.

A hand sank down on my bouncing knee.

Turning to Luke, who had taken the seat beside me against the door, he murmured, "Relax."

I bit the inside of my cheek. "That noticeable, huh?"

His eyes crinkled as he smiled. "Just a bit."

Sinking further into the seat, I sighed, rubbing my fingers into my temples. "I can't help it. I just know something is going to happen."

Luke curled his fingers with mine. "Perhaps you have a bit of precognition? It wouldn't be the first time a human had some latent abilities from some long-lost mage in their family lineage or something."

I gave him a stiff smile. Or something for sure.

By the time the car stopped, I was a ball of nerves and anxiety. The only positive side was I had no room for the other Eva to come out and play. Though, that could quickly change the moment I got out of the car.

All of the men piled out of the car, leaving me as the last one. Adam leaned down and held a hand out to me with an encouraging smile. "Can't hide in here all night. Let's go cause some chaos."

Against my better judgment, I slid my hand into his and allowed him to help me out from the safety of the car.

A line of mages with those sticks and flying eyes stood behind a red rope. It didn't keep them from trying to shove their sticks in our faces as we walked down a white carpet heading into the all-glass building before us.

"Master Adam, Master Adam. Isn't this the human from the tower?"

"Are you two an item now?"

"What do you have to say about the uprising in the Dakotas?"

Completely overwhelmed, I kept my mouth shut and watched as Adam waved them off with a simple "No comment."

"Freaking vultures," Blake muttered once we were all inside together.

"You'd think they'd have something better to do than hound us," Luke added on with a roll of his eyes and flashed a smile in my direction. "Though, I can't blame them. It's hard not to notice us with Eva here."

My cheeks burned as I smiled back at him. If they kept complimenting me so much, I was going to get a big head.

"Come along," Adam gestured toward the decorated opening inside the building, leading into a big open space.

There were all kinds of flowers decorating the place and little lights that hung in midair. I found my jaw falling open as I took in the wonderland of beauty all around me.

"Gorgeous, isn't it?" Adam leaned in to whisper in my ear.

"Yes," I breathed. "I've never seen anything like it."

"The building is completely made out of glass for transparency. But don't think that means the council would ever let any of those idiots outside see anything of importance." Adam jerked his head back toward the front door. "No, they'll make sure they are good and bored before the hour is up."

"Is that how we're going to feel?" I asked, rubbing my free hand down the length of my dress. "Because you wouldn't hear me complaining.

Adam suddenly grabbed my hand and spun me in place. "Not if I can help it."

I laughed and clung to him when he finally stopped. "What happened to making sure you're still available?"

Shrugging a shoulder, Adam avoided my gaze. "I can still play the part I need to play and have fun. Besides, you're here by the request of my grandfather in any case. So, if they have an issue with it, they can take it up with him."

His grandfather had asked for me? That's the first I'd heard of it. I thought Adam had wanted me to come. I'd thought a lot of things. Apparently, I had read the situation wrong.

Feeling a bit dejected, I couldn't hold onto the fun Adam had tried to inject into me. With my mind more reliable now, I felt the eyes on me. Mages filled the room to the brim. Some lined the sides while others sat at tables and chatted while eating from a long table with a variety of food. There was not a human in sight.

"I'm starving," Luke proclaimed, rubbing his stomach. "Let's get something to eat."

We all headed toward the food tables. While the men seemed at ease, excitedly talking to one another, my eyes kept sweeping the room, waiting for someone to comment on my presence.

I didn't have to wait long.

No sooner had we approached the long table of food than a male and female mage, who were obviously together by the way he had his hand low on her hip, approached us. It took me a moment, but I recognized them from the council of mages.

He had been the hungry eyed man next to the Arch Mage who had wanted to experiment on me. While her flaming red hair and slitted eyes were not easily forgotten. She had voted on putting me back in my tower for good.

My fingers tightened on Adam's arm.

"Master Adam," she hissed with a wicked grin, her slitted eyes sliding over to me.

"Mistress Ursula, Master Phineas." Adam inclined his head to them politely.

"I see you have brought your human with you. I almost didn't recognize her. She cleans up so well." The laughter in her voice was clearly at my expense.

Jaw tightening, I forced a smile to my face. "Thank you, you're too kind."

Taken back by the fact that I'd even dared to speak back to her, let alone lock eyes with her, she narrowed her snake-like eyes on me.

"It's clearly the work of Conjuror Blake," the man sneered, though while his words said one thing, his eyes were saying something else altogether. They licked over my exposed skin and made me wish I could go back to the house and take a thorough bath.

Blake snorted. "I hardly did anything at all. It's all, Eva."

I shot a grateful smile to Blake, who tipped a glass he had gotten from somewhere. I hoped it was some kind of alcohol because I needed something to get through this night without having an incident.

As if reading my mind, Luke produced a similar glass with bubbling pink liquid. "Here, you'll like this."

Happily, I sipped from my glass. Bubbles tickled my nose as I sighed. "Thank you."

"So, tell me, Eva," Ursula hissed, her golden-green eyes watching me with interest. "How have you been enjoying our world? Have you found your place yet?"

Drinking deeply from the glass, I thought about my answer. I wasn't sure if I was supposed to play the dutiful servant or speak my mind. Choosing the latter option, I tipped my head to the side. "As I told Adam," I purposely used his name without his title, "I do not understand why, with all the powers you mages possess, you even need humans to cook and clean for you? It seems like an easy task to me to simply wave your hand or whatever it is you mages do and have it done with."

Phineas threw his head back and laughed. "Silly human girl, have they taught you nothing of our ways? Our powers are not

205

toys. They aren't meant for such trivial things. Cooking, cleaning, and the like are beneath us. We should be focusing our attention on more important matters." His gaze seared through me. "Like discovering new anomalies such as yourself."

"And yet, they are alright for humans?" I had to stop talking. I could feel the other Eva pushing up against my mind. My words weren't entirely my own. Usually, I would have gone for the more defusing answer, not the controversial one.

Thankfully, Phineas took my answer in stride, grinning maniacally. "What else is there for a human to do?"

"Thank you for your insight, Master Phineas. Mistress Ursula." Adam inclined his head to them before gesturing his own glass off to the side. "You'll have to excuse us. I see my grandfather over there."

"Of course," Mistress Ursula hissed, observing me carefully.

"Ugh," I grumbled after we were out of earshot. "I hope the whole night isn't going to be like that."

Adam chuckled and handed me a plate. "I would count on it."

"I thought we were going to see your grandfather?" I asked while placing different kinds of food onto my plate. Each time I took something from a platter, another one appeared in its place.

So, that's how they kept the humans out of the room, I mused.

"We are. He's at the end of the line." Adam pointed toward the other side. "There's no reason we shouldn't take advantage of the situation."

Giggling, I continued down the line. Luke and Blake had much more on their plate than any of the other guests, and they made sure that every inch of my plate was full before I even got halfway down the table.

"Politics are hard work," Luke winked at me. "You have to keep your energy up."

We finally made it completely through the line, but Arch Mage Heizer was nowhere to be seen. Unfortunately, the she-bitch was there. She wasted no time plastering her body against Adam the moment we were free of the line.

Tonight, she wore a slinky black dress of shiny material. It seemed to be painted onto her skin and barely moved when she walked. Her long dark hair fell down her shoulders in waves, having not bothered to change her appearance much for the occasion.

"Adam," she purred, her ruby red lips pursed up in a pout. "I've been looking everywhere for you. Why didn't you come find me as soon as you arrived?"

Irritation ate at me as well as anticipation for what Adam might say. Would he tell her he was there with me? That's how Adam had made it seem to everyone else, and yet he didn't move to push her away from him.

"You know how it is," Adam sighed playfully. "I've been accosted by council members at every turn."

Rebecca made a cooing sound as she stroked his chest. "My poor baby, so much responsibility being the Arch Mage's grandson."

I'd like to say the other Eva was the one who was seething with jealousy and hurt, but it was ultimately me. My fingers tightened around the stem of my glass as I cleared my throat.

"Oh, yes," Adam cleared his throat and finally looked in my direction. "Eva, you remember Rebecca."

I inclined my head, giving her a full tooth smile. I didn't have to look in the mirror to know it wasn't a pleasant smile.

Rebecca didn't greet me the way the others had, she took one look at me and scowled, "What is she doing here?"

"My grandfather invited her."

I gaped at Adam. While that might be the truth, he wasn't even standing up for me. I knew he had to play a particular part, but this was ridiculous. Not bothering to excuse myself, I stepped away from them and found Zane and the others sitting at a nearby table.

"Distract me, please." I sat down between Zane and Blake. "I'm going to go full-on Queen Eva if I don't get away from Rebecca."

Blake snorted, shoving food into his mouth without looking at it.

"Can you even taste what you're eating?" I asked, jokingly at them.

Luke swallowed hard. "Of course. We eat the same things every year." He shrugged a shoulder. "No need to taste it."

I sat there with them eating off my plate as we chatted and pointed out the most ridiculous outfits. Blake had been right. I wasn't the strangest dressed one there. I swore there was even a woman covered in all feathers. They must have been stuck on with magic because I didn't see any clothing on the woman at all.

"Cleric Zane." A balding older mage approached the table with a small, beaten up black book in his hands.

"Ah, Cleric Vines." Zane shifted in his chair to greet the mage. "How are you?"

"Very well," Cleric Vines' gaze darted to me as he spoke but didn't comment. "I found the diary you were looking for."

"You did?" Zane's expression lit up, eagerness in his eyes.

Cleric Vines held out the book to him and chuckled. "It took quite a bit of digging, but I finally found it. The last known diary of the Queen of Phrygia from the fifteen hundreds."

My eyes widened, and a gasp slipped out before I could stop it. I hid it behind a cough and turned my eyes down to my food, pretending to be more interested in it than what they were saying.

Zane took the book from Cleric Vines with a smile of gratitude. "Thank you, this will definitely help with my research."

"If you don't mind me asking, what exactly are you looking for?"

"I'm sorry, that's classified. Mage client confidentiality, you understand," Zane explained politely.

"Oh, yes. Yes." Cleric Vines nodded. "Of course. Let me know if I can be of any help."

"I will. Thank you once again."

When the mage finally left, Zane turned to me. Before he could get a word out, I blurted out, "Is that about me? What does it say?"

Zane shook his head. "No, it's about Queen Snow."

Chapter 19

THE DIARY OF SNOW? The woman who had put me in that tower? The one who thought I had done such horrible things that I had to be punished for eternity?

I wasn't sure I wanted to read it.

And yet, I still reached for the book.

Zane held it out of my grasp with a small frown. "Perhaps, I should read it first...there might be things you don't want to see in here."

"No," I shook my head and held my hand out, "if there is something that bad about me in there, I need to read it for myself."

Exchanging a look with the others, Zane relented and handed it over. "If you insist, but I really wish you would wait until we return home before reading it. There might be upsetting passages."

"I'll be fine," I insisted and flipped to the first page. Snow's writing was tight and lacked much of the flourish I'd seen on many of the written scrolls and books. It made it easier to read, and yet it was as if she wasn't herself when writing it. It certainly didn't represent the woman I'd seen in my dreams.

Pushing the background noise outof my head, I bent over the book, scouring it for anything of use. There were many passages describing parties Snow went to and musings about her tutors. There were plenty of rants about her stepmother - me - I apparently was a despicable person only capable of loving myself.

No surprise there.

"Find anything yet?" Luke leaned over the table to see the words.

Shaking my head, I sighed. "No. Not yet. Just a bunch of boring complaints or daydreaming. Wait." I paused on a page near the end of the book. I'd basically just been flipping them now to see if anything stood out.

Ferdinand. She mentioned the prince here.

I do not know who may read this, but it is imperative that I write it down. I have been careful not to mention my affair with Prince Ferdinand in here, but now that we are married, I am able to speak more freely.

Today was to be my honeymoon.

The words were smeared here as if moisture had touched the page. Had she been crying? The thought of it made my heart clench tight. Even though Snow had been the one to lock me up, I didn't wish pain on her. Being a person on the outside looking in, I could see how she would find her stepmother to be the villain.

I turned back to the passage.

Instead of being in my wedding bliss, I am burying my husband. Prince Ferdinand.

We were not allowed to show his body to the people for them to pay their respects. There wasn't much of him left to mourn. Eva has greatly cursed me. The last sight of my loving and wonderful Ferdinand was of blood and horror. I can still see it now.

His lovely face, torn to pieces. Those piercing eyes of his falling from their place in his head. I emptied my stomach the moment I saw him before wailing in horror and sadness. How could someone be so cruel? Be so vicious? It had been my wedding night, and she had stolen it away from me.

Everything. She has stolen everything.

I cannot provide it yet, but I know my father did not die of natural causes. He was a champion hunter. There was no way he was flung from his horse and run down by some common stag. She had to have had a hand in it: her and her magicks.

"Eva," Zane said my name softly and placed his hand on mine. "Are you alright?"

I swallowed hard and shook my head. "No. I'm not." I closed the book with a snap. "I think I'll wait and read the rest later."

"Here." Blake pushed his glass in front of me. "Drink."

Happily accepting it, I downed the glass quickly and breathed out slowly. The other didn't ask me about what I read but waited for me to speak.

Sitting the glass back down, my eyes burned with tears of frustration and anger. I lifted my head and closed them tightly, willing them back. This was not the time or place.

"What's wrong with the human?" Rebecca's haughty voice filled my ears. "Not able to cut it in the mage's world? That's alright, dear. Not many can. You don't belong here after all."

My jaw clenched. I lowered my head and glared at Rebecca across the table, where she and Adam were taking a seat at the table. "I'm doing just fine. Better than you even."

"I don't see how that's possible," Rebecca grinned maliciously. "You don't have magic. I have magic, and Adam here has accepted my proposal of marriage."

Luke choked on his drink.

Blake hurried to pat him on the back, while the rest of us stared at them in shock.

Adam's face was perfectly neutral. He gave nothing away of what or why he would have done such a thing.

"Adam, is this true?" Zane prodded, clearly as surprised as the rest of us.

Lifting a shoulder, Adam answered in an even voice, "It was the logical thing to do. I cannot hope to gain the Arch Mage position without having taken a wife, and Rebecca and I have been involved before. She was a logical choice."

"And you're alright with him using you for political purposes?" Luke asked what we all were thinking.

Rebecca smirked. "What makes you think I do not have political aspirations of my own?"

What happened next was so sudden, I couldn't have possibly stopped it. Their answers were so idiotic. So painfully unaware of how ridiculous they sounded all the while, breaking my heart into a million little pieces. It only served them right.

My hand shot up, and a ball of flame shot out. Adam barely had the time to throw up a shield of magic in front of them both, absorbing the fire into its surface.

The entire table stared at me in a mixture of horror and disbelief.

"Eva?" Zane was the first to speak. "You have magic?

Luke watched me with concern. "Why didn't you tell us? When did you know?"

Rebecca though, was not interested in what I had to say. "She's obviously been hiding it, the filthy little half breed." She stood to her feet and pointed her finger at me, her voice rising as she screeched. "She should be put down now."

"Now, Rebecca," Adam wrapped his arms around her waist and drew her to him. "We don't know that. She could be late to her powers is all. Most mage children smell of human just the same."

I wished. Things would have been simpler if that were the case.

Rebecca agreed with me. "There has never been a case of a mage coming into their powers this late in life." Her eyes narrowed on me. "Now, I know why they locked you away. No mage should ever lower themselves to bed a human, let alone breed with one. You disgust me."

My chair flew back on its own, and my skin tingled with power. Every word she had said was the exact same as a mage had told the other Eva so long ago. Hearing those words alone were enough to give her a handhold to take over.

"You're right." A low sultry voice came from my mouth, so much more confident than I ever was. "I should be locked away. It was your kind who locked me away in the first place. One would think you would have the intelligence to remember why."

A fireball blasted from my hand, hitting the table of food. People screamed, and food went flying everywhere. Another shot crashed into the glass wall, shattering it.

"That glass was enchanted. Completely magic proof. She shouldn't have been able to do that." Zane's eyes widened, fear flickering over his face.

"Stop her!" someone called out, and mages rushed me.

The other Eva didn't care, though. She cast a spell capturing them in a slimy green substance that grew around them until they couldn't move. Another spell sent three of them flying across the room and through the smashed glass.

The men at my table were the only ones not trying to stop me.

"Eva," Luke stepped toward me. "You have to stop this. You're not her. You're you."

The other Eva gave him a passing look before turning away from him. "Your Eva isn't home right now. Please try again later." A cackled filled with delight fell from my mouth as mage upon mage was thrown to the ground and knocked out. Finally, a path was cleared around me. A twist of my hand and the book disappeared. Somewhere in the back of my mind, I knew she had stuck it in a sort of air pocket. Safe, but out of the way. The other Eva grabbed the sides of my skirt and walked away from my men.

Can't have them stopping me, now can we? Her voice rang out clearly in my head, and I tried to argue back with her, but she simply laughed at me.

"Where do you think you're going?" Master Tuck appeared in my path. "You owe your life to us. We got you out of that tower, and we can put you back."

Instead of using magic to get rid of him, the other Eva grabbed him by the front of his clothes and pulled him close. "I owe nothing to you people. You are nothing." I felt the magic inside of me swell up before it happened. I tried to cry out. To make her stop, but I couldn't.

Master Tuck disintegrated into a million little pieces before my very eyes. The only thing the other Eva did was brush her hands and clothes off before continuing on her way. After seeing her little display, the mages were reluctant to attack her, moving out of her way faster than she could walk by. The other Eva laughed and grinned victoriously.

The group of mages with their sticks and floating eyes were still standing outside the building. Having seen what had happened inside, their eyes were wide with terror and fascination.

"What? No questions for me?" The other Eva taunted them and fingers the air with her nails.

Only one person had the nerve to speak. A small man with a wrinkled face and pale blue eyes stared up at me with wonder. "Who are you?"

"I am Eva, but you may call me, my queen." The other Eva waved her hand, and magic shot out. Every single one of them bowed before her, whether they wanted to or not.

Happy with herself, the other Eva turned from what the others called the vultures and moved to walk away. Except stopped. My eyes locked on the tower in the distance peeking up out of the dead trees of the old Central Park.

My body turned toward the tower, heading across the streets without a care for the cars I was stopping. Strangely enough, flowers bloomed where I walked as we passed the gates of the park. Green leaves sprouted on long since dead trees and grass grew out of the dry ground.

I had never liked dead things. Even as a child, my mother would bring me to the gardens to heal a bird or a plant. It was how they found out I had powers. How King Midas had found me for his collection of pretty things.

The park passed by me until I came to the base of my tower. The other Eva stared up at it for a long time and then the magic inside built. Hotter and hotter, it grew until I felt as if I might burn up from the inside out. Then it unleashed.

The tower exploded. Bricks flew across the air, and flames licked the sky. The color of the fire changed from red to yellow to blue, turning the tower into a small pile of ash and soot within minutes.

"There." The other Eva sighed. "Now, no one can trap us in there again."

All at once, she left my body, and I collapsed on the ground, shaking. What had I done? I stared down at my hands in horror. I had killed someone. Not just in a past life but only a few moments ago. Master Tuck was there and then...he was just gone.

Tears streamed down my face as I knelt on the still blooming ground. Sirens blared in the distance, but I didn't care. Let them take me away. I deserved it.

I vaguely remembered hands grabbing me from under my arms. They tried to put some kind of braces on my arms, but someone commented, "She's gone. She's not a threat anymore."

Huffing out a laugh, I disagreed with them. I was a threat. I had always been a threat...to everyone.

Chapter 20

THE ROOM THEY HAD thrown me in was more of a cell than anything I'd been locked in. Not even my tower was this damp and dark. For three days, I had sat in this cell, only occasionally having a tray of cold slop slid into a panel.

The first day, I had refused it, unable to choke it down after being spoiled on so much rich food. The others would come for me.

I had chanted it over and over again as I waited in my cell. They wouldn't leave me here. They couldn't.

But look at what you've done. Why would they come for you? The other Eva taunted me.

By the second day, my hope began to diminish. There was a drip somewhere I couldn't find no matter how much I searched the pipes of the small dingy sink next to the foul-smelling toilet. When they gave me my daily tray of slop, I ate it like a wild animal unable to care what it tasted like as long as it quelled the burning in my gut.

On the third day, I couldn't bear it anymore. I banged on the door and screamed until my throat burned. This was worse than the tower had ever been. At least then, I'd been spelled in a room I could see. The darkness ate at my mind. Not being able to see anything but hearing every single movement drove me mad.

Something skittered across the floor and brushed my foot. I stifled a scream. My bare feet on the slimy floor made my shoulders bunch with disgust. I scrambled up onto the thin mattress of the rickety bed.

Wrapping my arms around my knees, I leaned my head back against the cold stone wall. As much as I hated the cell, I deserved it. Queen Eva deserved it. She had slaughtered the man she loved and the man she was married to as well as Master Tuck and probably hundreds of other mages.

The killing itself was evil enough, but the way she had reveled in it—the laughter. I could hear it now, bouncing off the walls of my cell. It mocked me. It told me this was me. Not Queen Eva. We were one and the same person. I couldn't separate her actions from mine anymore.

Lifting my hands up, I could see the blood on them in my mind. I'd tried to wash them in the freezing water of the sink, but it wouldn't go away.

Because it's not there. We're losing our minds again.

No. I refused it. I wouldn't go back there again. I couldn't. Someone would come for me. They couldn't keep me in here forever.

Don't be so naive. No one is coming for us. They didn't the first time, why should they now?

"Shut up," I grabbed at my head, trying to shove the other Eva's voice away. She had been more prominent in my mind ever since I found out who I really was.

When I slept, she filled my mind with memories of what the mages had done to my mother. How they had butchered her in front of our whole town as an example of what would happen to anyone who dared defy them.

While awake, she taunted me with how stupid I was to think the mages would accept me. Even love me. I was nothing to them—a human and worthless.

"This is your fault," I shouted at her. "You get us out."

Of course, she didn't answer that one. She was happy to reveal her powers to a room full of mages because a single woman made a rude comment but use them to free us? I laughed bitterly at the irony of it all.

I jerked as the door opened abruptly. I squinted against the painful light pouring into the room.

"Stay where you are," a harsh voice demanded. Then a figure filled the door, and suddenly the room was filled with light.

Once my eyes adjusted to the light, I realized the cell was even more disgusting than what I thought. For a brief moment, I wished to be blinded by the darkness once more. I closed my eyes against the light and waited for them to do whatever it was they were bothering me for. If they weren't letting me out, I didn't want to know.

There was a clank of metal and then some rustling before the door shut once more. This time the light remained.

Opening my eyes once more, I searched the room for what they had done. The clank had been a chair being set down by the door. On top of the chair, laid out ever so nicely, was a gorgeous sapphire-colored dress with matching shoes seated at its feet.

Hesitantly, I dropped my legs and moved to the edge of the bed. Was this a trick? What was the point of giving me something so elegant while I was covered in dirt and grime? The dress I'd worn from the Gala was unrecognizable now, it's skirts smooshed out of shape and the pale violet of the material now a dirty brown.

As if knowing my thoughts, a portion of the wall clicked and pushed into the wall before sliding to the side. In its place, a pipe came out with a showerhead. The water began to spray out without me doing anything. A drain I hadn't noticed before was embedded into the ground below it.

Not having to be told twice. I hurried off the bed and stripped out of my dirty rags.

The water was cool but not freezing like the sink. I didn't have any soap, but I scrubbed my skin and hair as much as possible before the water switched off.

With a yelp, wind came out of nowhere and blew on me in an almost too hot spray, drying my skin and hair viciously. I turned my back to it, unable to breathe with how hard it was blowing. Finally, when it stopped, I sighed and moved to the clothes.

It took no time at all to get dressed in the simple, yet elegant gown and slip into the low-heeled shoes. I walked over to the sink, where I now could see a murky mirror stuck to the wall. My cheeks were a little less full than before, and my hair was frizzy because of the wind, but if someone saw me on the street, they would never know that I had been locked up for three days.

A part of me didn't trust the new clothes and the shower. Someone wanted something from me, and they wanted to make sure that I was desperate enough to take what they offered.

And yet...

Another part of me hoped it was one of the men in my life who were here to save me...again.

Doubtful.

"Shut it," I clipped back with a snarl. "You're going to behave while I get us out of this."

Or what?

I was saved from having to answer her when the door opened again once more. My shoulders stiffened, and I was almost afraid to turn around. Finally, summoning up my courage, I slowly turned to find the last person I ever expected to see standing in my jail cell.

"My queen, it's so wonderful to have you back," Rebecca curtsied deeply. "At long last."

About the Author

Erin Bedford is an otaku, recovering coffee addict, and Legend of Zelda fanatic. Her brain is so full of stories that need to be told that she must get them out or explode into a million screaming chibis. Obsessed with fairy tales and bad boys, she hasn't found a story she can't twist to match her deviant mind full of innuendos, snarky humor, and dream guys.

On the outside, she's a work from home mom and bookbinger. One the inside, she's a thirteen-year-old boy screaming to get out and tell you the pervy joke they found online. As an ex-computer programmer, she dreams of one day combining her love for writing and college credits to make the ultimate video game!

Until then, when she's not writing, Erin is devouring as many books as possible on her quest to have the biggest book gut of all time. She's written over thirty books, ranging from paranormal romance, urban fantasy, and even scifi romance.

Come chat me up!
www.erinbedford.com
Facebook.com/erinrbedford
twitter.com/erin_bedford
Don't forget to follow me on Goodreads,
Pinterest, Instagram, and YouTube!

**Want to be the first to know about my
new releases?**
Erinbedford.com/newsletter

www.ingramcontent.com/pod-product-compliance
Lightning Source LLC
Chambersburg PA
CBHW070930190726
48292CB00004B/1187